THE SCARECROW MYSTERY

THE TED WILFORD SERIES

THE SCARECROW MYSTERY

NORVIN PALLAS

WILDSIDE PRESS

To
Les, Dan, and Greg.

CHAPTER 1

NEW YEAR'S PLANS

"GET YOUR INVITATION YET TO THE NEW Year's Eve shindig?"

This question was asked by Nelson Morgan, who was lying on the bed leafing through the pages of a sports magazine.

It was addressed to his close friend, Ted Wilford, who was sitting in front of the desk, pasting items from the Forestdale semiweekly newspaper, the *Town Crier,* in a little scrapbook. Ted had once been a "stringer" for the paper, and it had been necessary for him to keep track of all his published writings because he was paid by the printed inch. Now that he was paid a salary when he worked on the paper during his college vacations, he didn't have to keep track of all items, but he liked to do it just the same. These clippings reminded him of many little incidents and adventures he might otherwise have forgotten. Besides, he liked to imagine that he could detect some improvement in his work.

"Got it," he answered briefly.

"I'm going with Sue Anderson," Nelson went on. "I wonder how she happened to ask me? I've never been out with her before."

"Maybe *that's* the reason," Ted retorted sarcastically.

Nelson ignored this remark. "And of course you're going with Margaret Lake."

"What do you mean, 'of course'?" Ted came back.

"Because nobody'd dare to break up *that* twosome. Anyway, a treasure hunt ought to be fun."

"A scavenger hunt," Ted corrected him.

"What's the difference?"

"For a treasure hunt you get clues to follow, until you finally reach the treasure. In a scavenger hunt you get a list of things to bring back."

"Sounds like almost the same thing to me. You coming along in my car?"

"No, Mr. Lake says I can borrow his."

"Lucky dog! I've never been able to figure out why everybody trusts you so much. All I can say is that you've never yet got me into any *little* trouble."

Ted turned back to his string book, frowning over a minor problem. "I wonder whether I wrote this story or not?"

"Don't you know?" asked Nelson, puzzled.

"Not exactly. As I remember, somebody phoned in the story, and I wrote it down almost the way I got it. Does that make it my story or not?"

"Sure, it does. You're the one who put it down on paper."

"I put this other one down on paper, too. But we were short of space, and Mr. Dobson blue-penciled most of it and rewrote the lead. When you work on a newspaper, you don't exactly write a story. It becomes more of a partnership."

"Then who cares whether you wrote it or not?" Nelson demanded.

"Nobody else, I guess, and maybe a year from now I won't care, either."

He decided not to include these clippings in his book, closed it up, and put away the scissors and paste. Nelson tossed aside the sports magazine, sat up on the edge of Ted's bed, and stretched.

"Sure is dull this time of year—I mean in sports. I wish I were about three inches taller so I could try out for the basketball team."

"You're playing intramural basketball. That's fun, isn't it?"

"Oh, I suppose it's fun, all right, but you'll never get your name in the paper that way. We're lucky if the college paper prints the score."

"Well, what's so wonderful about getting your name in the paper? I know a lot of people who have, and wished they hadn't."

"Look who's talking! Mr. Dobson's fair-haired boy, who can get his name printed twice a week, if he wants to."

"What do you mean? Just because I write a few little things for the paper, do you think Mr. Dobson gives me a by-line any time I ask for it? Things aren't that easy."

"Well, maybe you don't every week, but you've had your share."

"You must mean on the high-school paper. You know how many by-lines I've had on the *Town Crier?* Count 'em up on the fingers on your hand, and when you get to none—stop!"

"That right?" said Nelson lamely. "I thought I remembered seeing a few of them."

"Sure, you did, and so did I—the way a thirsty man on a desert sees a lake in the distance. By-lines don't come often with Mr. Dobson, and that big story is still in the faraway future."

"Well, then, getting one is a good thing to put on your list of New Year's resolutions."

"Is it? That big story depends a lot on luck, and I don't see how you can say, 'I'm resolved to be lucky this year.' I'd like to see your list, though. I'll bet it's something."

"Oh, I didn't make up any list—not really. I know something I'd like to do, though. I want to win some kind of competition with my camera. There are lots of different contests, and I'm going to see if I can't come up with something."

"Landscapes?"

"No, I don't think so. There I'm up against fellows with a lot better equipment and a lot more experience than I've got. I'm thinking of the candid field. If you're there at the right time, you can always beat out the fellow who isn't there, no matter what kind of camera he's got."

"That takes a lot of luck, too," Ted pointed out.

"Well, maybe. I don't suppose a person could live without luck. But you have to be awake when your opportunity comes along. Let's see. This is Wednesday night. Thursday, Friday, Saturday, Sunday. Four days more before I have to start being wide-awake, according to my resolution."

"You aren't going to be very wide-awake on Monday if we're out till two-thirty."

"No—well, then, Monday to rest up, and Tuesday we'll start back for college, bright and early."

"Anyway, early," Ted agreed.

They were interrupted by the ring of the telephone downstairs, and Ted listened to see if it was for him. In a few moments his mother called upstairs.

"Ted, it's Mr. Dobson."

"Coming." He started to leave the room. "Want to wait, Nel?"

"Oh, don't mind me. I haven't looked through your photography books for a long time, and I might pick up some pointers. Don't hurry."

"Mr. Dobson's never long-winded. I'll be right back."

Picking up the phone, Ted wondered what his editor might want. He hoped he hadn't pulled some boner. Although Mr. Dobson was a very considerate man, he never put up with slipshod work.

"Hello, Mr. Dobson."

"Hello, Ted. Something has come along that I didn't know about earlier. I've just learned that Mr. Prentice—you know, Albert Prentice, head of the transit union—will be in Stanton tomorrow. Of course he'll be here in Forestdale for the court hearing on Friday morning, but that makes it too late for our Friday issue. I thought if we could get an interview with him tomorrow morning, it might give us something to peg a story on."

"You mean a telephone interview?"

"Well, no, Ted. I prefer a personal interview when the matter is important enough, and this one is."

"Then you want me to run down to Stanton tomorrow morning, Mr. Dobson?"

"I wish you would, Ted. You know how difficult it is for me to get away on a Thursday morning, and the two holidays have played hob with our printing schedule already. Do you suppose Nelson would drive you?"

"He's here now. Hold on, and I'll ask him."

Ted went to the foot of the stairs and called up to Nelson. "Want to drive down to Stanton in the morning?"

"Sure. O.K. by me," Nelson answered, and started downstairs to hear what it was all about.

"Yes, he will, Mr. Dobson."

"Fine! It makes it more convenient for me if I can keep my car here, and of course we'll pay Nelson the usual expense allowance and hourly rate. I've already arranged for the interview at nine o'clock at the Marquette Hotel."

Suddenly Ted began to feel a little nervous. Interviewing people wasn't exactly a novelty to him, for he frequently made telephone calls at the *Town Crier* office, and lately, during the absence of Carl

Allison, the newspaper's regular reporter, he had interviewed a few of the townspeople. But this was different. Mr. Prentice was a stranger, and this was a very important story. It wasn't quite as easy as walking up to the fire chief, whom he had known for years, and asking if there was anything new.

"Any special instructions, Mr. Dobson?"

"You're familiar with the general situation, Ted. Of course the most important question is whether or not there's going to be a trucking strike, and what form it might take, though I don't think you'll be able to get a clear-cut answer to that. And of course everybody's interested in whether there's any truth to the charge that the union has a kick-back arrangement with Jed Myers, even though he's now serving a prison sentence for extortion. That may come out in the court hearing Friday morning, but Mr. Prentice's comments would be interesting right now.

"I've looked through our files here at the office, but there doesn't seem to be anything that would help you. The city daily paper would be more useful. Do you have back copies of it there?"

"I'm pretty sure I do, but if not, I'll find them somewhere."

"Then check back through the last few weeks and get as familiar with the situation as you can. It doesn't pay to go into an interview poorly informed. That's about all I can think of, Ted. Phone in your story as soon as you get it."

"All right, Mr. Dobson, I'll do my best."

Hanging up the phone, Ted turned to Nelson. "Nine o'clock interview," he informed him. "That means we get on the road by six-thirty."

"Six-thirty! Then what's the use of going to bed at all?"

"Well, I don't suppose you have to come yourself. I could rent your car. Or maybe I ought to think about getting a car of my own. You must get tired of acting as my chauffeur."

Nelson looked crestfallen. "Oh, come on, Ted. You wouldn't do that, would you, and spoil all my fun?" He thought about it a moment. "But maybe Mr. Dobson's going to get tired of this arrangement before long. Why should he pay two of us, when one man could do it alone?"

"Don't worry about Mr. Dobson. He's pretty shrewd. He knows you've come in mighty handy several times, apart from driving the car."

Nelson grinned. "All right, then. Six-thirty. What are you going to do now, Ted?"

"I want to look through the old papers in the basement, and pick up all I can on this trucking strike. Want to help me?"

"Heck, no! That sounds like work. Anyway, it looks to me like these strikes are phony."

"How do you mean?"

"Almost every time there's a strike, or the threat of a strike, both management and labor know ahead of time on just about what terms they're going to have to settle. But they both have to show their muscles, make a lot of threats, and maybe go out on a short strike to show they really meant it. They couldn't just *quietly* come to an agreement. The public might not realize how important the trucking business is, unless the trucks didn't move every now and then, or there was a threat that they wouldn't. So labor asks for twice as much as it expects to get, and management concedes only half as much as it knows it will have to concede. Then after they've had a big enough rumpus, they settle on the same terms they could have at the beginning, and everybody's happy. The union officers can show their members what they got for them, and management can show the stockholders how much it saved them, and they've all gotten their names in the papers."

"You think that's all there is to it—just acting important?"

"Well, no." Nelson looked thoughtful. "I think sometimes they really do want a strike—both management and labor. Maybe the inventory's running high, and management would like to cut down without actually firing anyone. And maybe labor wouldn't mind a little extra holiday—have you noticed how many contracts expire just when the hunting or fishing seasons open?"

"Then you think there won't be any strike, because this isn't the hunting or fishing season?"

"I didn't say that. I suppose the trucking business *does* slow down after Christmas, and I suppose the workers wouldn't mind a little extra time off around the holidays." He studied Ted's face for a moment. "Which side are you on—management or labor?"

Ted laughed. "I'd like to say I'm on the side of truth, but sometimes I wonder if there is such a thing. It often seems to be pretty much a matter of where you're standing. After all, your finger looks bigger than a barn, if you hold it right in front of your eyes."

"But a finger *isn't* bigger than a barn, Ted, no matter how it looks."

"Maybe not. But if somebody pinches it, that finger's going to *hurt* more than the barn."

"How about it, Ted—do you think the unions get a fair shake in the papers? They often complain that they don't."

"I know Mr. Dobson always tries to be fair, and I suppose most of the other papers do, too. But I think that often the unions get bad publicity due to something that really isn't anybody's fault. Usually it's the employers who want to keep things going the way they are, and it's the union that wants to improve things for themselves. No matter how fairly you write up that story, the casual reader is apt to blame labor. As he sees it, things *were* going along smoothly, and the people who want to change things are the trouble-makers."

Nelson agreed and then decided he'd better get going if he wanted to see a television program he liked. Ted retired to the basement, where he spent a couple of hours doing some important homework.

CHAPTER 2

A GOOD JOB WELL DONE

WHEN THEY HAD GOT TO STANTON NEXT MORNing, Ted had no trouble reaching Mr. Prentice at the hotel, and was told to come up to room 208.

"Want me to come with you, Ted?" asked Nelson.

"No, better not. I look young enough as it is, and Mr. Prentice might get the wrong impression if he thinks I need someone along to give me support—even if I do. I'll try not to be any longer than I can help."

Mr. Prentice opened the door at Ted's ring.

"I'm Ted Wilford, from the Forestdale *Town Crier*."

"Come on in, Ted. I have to leave for an appointment in half an hour, but that should give us enough time. Take off your coat and sit down. Coffee?"

"No, thanks," said Ted, settling himself in a chair. He had a note-book and pencil in his pocket, but did not produce them right away. He had often heard that some people get upset if they think every-thing they say is being taken down.

Ted had briefed himself as carefully as he could on the strike situ-ation, but it was such a complicated affair that it was hard to know just where to begin. Finally he decided it was best to go directly to the main point.

"Mr. Prentice, do you think there is going to be a trucking strike?"

The union leader hesitated. "The union isn't going to call a strike, Ted, as long as our contract is being observed. But if these violations of our contract go on, it's quite possible that the executive council will call for a strike vote."

"The owners claim that it's the union that is breaking the con-tract."

"That isn't true, of course. We're not completely satisfied with the present contract, but we're willing to work under it until it expires. There have been only a few minor violations when, due to illness, we haven't been able to get workers on the job."

"Isn't it true that the absentee rate has been abnormally high?"

"It always is, in winter."

"But they have statistics to show that the absentee rate is more than twice as high as the rate for the same period in previous years."

"That's just the kind of insinuation I don't like, Ted. You can't judge by previous years. Colds and flu can hit a peak any time between November and March. This year it happened to hit at the end of December. I'm not trying to whitewash labor. We have our occasional goldbrickers, just the way any organization does. But if a man claims he's ill, I'm willing to believe he's ill, unless I see a doctor's certificate to the contrary.

"The real trouble," added Mr. Prentice bitterly, "is that the employers wouldn't believe us even if we presented them with a whole bushel of doctors' certificates."

"If a contract is being broken, wouldn't a court be the proper place to settle it?"

"What kind of court did you have in mind? A broken contract is a civil offense, not a criminal, and lawsuits can drag through the courts for months or years."

"Have you any reason to think your men may start some trouble this weekend?"

"Aren't you prejudging the case, Ted? If there's trouble, why does it prove that *our* men started it?"

"But there have been incidents in which individual workers have defied their leaders. If the union can't control its own membership, then why does it have any right to expect a contract?"

"I'm not angry at your questions, Ted, because I realize you're only doing your job. What burns me up is that the same statement is made by responsible men who ought to know better. If the union leaders sincerely try to live up to the contract, they can't be held to blame for the actions of an irresponsible few. If individual members have broken the contract, or broken the law in some way, let them be punished as individuals."

"Wouldn't that be awfully hard to pin down?"

"Perhaps it would, but I don't see where the employers have a legitimate complaint as long as the union leaders, and the vast majority of the union members, are obeying the contract. As for the others, the union can handle them with its own methods."

"Apparently the employers don't believe they are effective enough."

"No, because they're anxious to blame the *whole* union."

"What if a small group of men went out on strike, what would the union do about it?"

"The officers would make every effort to get them back to work, as long as the strike did not represent the vote of any local unit. Of course if a local did call a legitimate strike, then we'd have to approve it."

"Suppose the strike spread to other locals, how far might it reach?"

"As far as the area covered by the contracts in question—that is, this entire half of the state."

"Even if the employers were violating the contract, couldn't the men continue working until court action could be started?"

"Ted, we've learned through long, bitter experience that without a legitimate contract, it is better to walk out."

Although Mr. Prentice had not directly answered his most important question, Ted felt he had the answer. If the union thought there were contract violations, there was going to be a strike, probably over the coming weekend, which would involve this whole section of the state. But there was still the matter of the pending court hearing.

"Do you intend to produce the union records for the court hearing tomorrow morning in Forestdale?"

"Of course I do. That's what the judge asked for, and that's what he's going to get. I have a microfilm of the files for the period concerned."

"As I understand it, one of the principal charges is a connection between certain members of the union and certain racketeers. Do you think there will be anything in the records to prove it?"

"I most certainly do not!"

"Then you deny you've ever had any dealings with Jed Myers?"

"I deny it now, and I'll deny it emphatically tomorrow morning on the witness stand."

"Is it possible that any other officer in the union had such dealings?"

Mr. Prentice's face flushed a deep red. "If there had been any arrangement with Jed Myers, I don't see why I wouldn't have known about it."

But he was less certain and more blustery. Ted thought: He thinks not, but he isn't sure. Mr. Prentice couldn't be positive that someone might not have been involved with Jed Myers, and it seemed to Ted he was afraid it might come out at the court hearing. Ted felt it time to draw the interview to a close.

"Thank you, Mr. Prentice. I think that gives me everything I need, and I appreciate your giving me so much of your time."

"Not at all, Ted. I'm not asking for favors, but just give us a fair break in your story. Phone from here if you want to, and I've got a portable typewriter over by that table you're welcome to use. I'm going out and will leave you to it."

"I have a friend waiting in the lobby who drove me down. All right if he comes up?"

"Sure. By the way, Ted, if you're still here when I get back, perhaps we could drive up to Forestdale together. It'll be too early for lunch, but we could stop somewhere along the road."

"That would be fine, Mr. Prentice. I'll wait as long as I can."

"This is all right," Nelson remarked after he joined Ted, "but it's not the best suite in the place, and Mr. Prentice wasn't dressed very well. It doesn't look like he's getting rich on union money."

"No, he struck me as a very honest person, but of course he doesn't tell everything he knows. I don't think he'd concede one inch, if he thought he was right. I hope we have lunch together. I'd like to get a little stronger impression of him."

"What goes, Ted? You sound like you expected to *stay* on the story. We're going back to college, remember?"

"That's right. Well, maybe Mr. Dobson will let me cover the court hearing tomorrow morning. But right now I want to get what he said down on paper, before I lose it."

For nearly an hour the keys clacked rhythmically. Of course it wasn't possible for Ted to say that there was going to be a strike, which was really only his opinion, but the reader was certain to get the idea that a strike was a strong possibility. Ted supposed that

Mr. Dobson would probably put a headline over the story reading: *TRUCKING STRIKE LOOMS,* or something like that.

When Ted felt satisfied he'd done the best he could in the time he had, he put through a collect call to the *Town Crier* office. Miss Monroe answered.

"Oh, Ted. Wait till I put on my earphones, and I'll type the story as you read it. Mr. Dobson's listening on the other phone. He wants to hear it, too."

"All right, Ted, go ahead," said Mr. Dobson's voice.

Ted read his story slowly enough for Miss Monroe to copy it. When he had finished, Mr. Dobson had a few questions. Fortunately Ted was able to give him the additional information he wanted.

Ted knew that the editor was pleased, though his voice was crisp. They were generally rushed on deadline morning, but after noon they could all relax a little.

"Thanks, Ted," the editor commended him. "It's a good job well done. There's no great hurry getting back, but if you're here before two, Miss Monroe will be able to get to the bank before it closes."

They hung up, and Ted felt suddenly relieved and almost carefree.

CHAPTER 3

THE LONG ROAD HOME

"WELL, WHAT DO WE DO NOW?" ASKED NELSON impatiently.

"Wait for Mr. Prentice, if we can. I don't have to get back till two, so we can wait till eleven or so."

"Your story was written from the standpoint of the labor union, Ted. You think that's fair?"

"The paper will carry an interview with Mr. Abbott, too. He's the largest of the private owners. Mr. Dobson took care of that part of it."

"Know something?" said Nelson suddenly. "If there *is* a strike and trouble develops, I'm going to keep my camera handy. Maybe this is the sort of thing I'm looking for—you know, something to enter in a contest. A nice, big, juicy riot, and me the only one on the spot with a camera."

"Well, I hope you get out of it alive."

"Yeah," said Nelson gloomily.

"I wonder," said Ted meditatively, his thoughts shooting off on a tangent, "about Mr. Prentice. He's such a fluent talker that you get the impression he must know what he's talking about. But I wonder about his statistics. That seems to be the key to the whole situation."

"From what I've heard about statistics," Nelson put in, "both sides quote the same figures to prove that they're right! You can prove almost anything you want to with figures."

"Oh, I imagine statistics are all right, as long as you know what it is you've got. You might put all men between the ages of twenty and twenty-nine in one group, and between the ages of thirty and thirty-nine in another group. What you've got to remember is that a man of twenty-nine is closer in age to a man of thirty from the other group than he is to a man of twenty in his own group."

"But he'd be just as close to a man of twenty-eight as he would to a man of thirty," Nelson observed.

"Yes. Well, I suppose it all depends on what you're trying to prove. If you were going to place a man, a frog, and a stone in two groups, how would you do it?"

"You'd have to put the man and the frog in the same group, wouldn't you?"

"That's because the fact of being alive seems the most important thing to us. But if you were calculating the load on an airplane, you might put the man and the stone in the same group, and hardly bother with the weight of the frog."

"Maybe it's a little stone that only weighs as much as the frog," said Nelson with a grin, "and so where are you?"

"I guess I'm right back wondering whether I ought to sign up for statistics or calculus next term."

"Statistics would be more useful in journalism, wouldn't it?"

"I suppose so, but I'd hate to by-pass calculus and find out later that it's got something I need."

"Why don't you ask your friend, Mr. Halliday?" Nelson suggested. "He'd have all that right at his fingertips. And he must know what he's talking about, or he wouldn't be running the most successful investment business in the county."

"You know, I just might do that. He's always been a good friend. That time years ago when our family ran into some tough sledding and he pushed through a mortgage extension for us—well, that's the sort of thing you never forget. I guess I've been kind of leaning on him for advice ever since."

* * * *

Mr. Prentice came back before eleven o'clock, saving them the problem of deciding how long to wait. He seemed glad to see them.

"Give me just five minutes more, boys, and I'll be packed and ready to go."

Within this time limit he emerged from his bedroom carrying two suitcases. He checked through the desk, found nothing there he had forgotten, and announced himself ready to leave. Nelson took one of the suitcases, and Ted the portable typewriter. Downstairs, it was only a matter of minutes to check out at the registration desk, and they left for the hotel's parking lot. Mr. Prentice's car turned out to be a medium-priced model, three years old, so once again it was apparent he wasn't putting on the dog.

Out on the main highway, Nelson let Mr. Prentice take the lead. "I don't know how fast he wants to go," he explained.

"Maybe he'll go so fast you won't be able to keep up." Ted grinned.

"Don't worry about that. If he stays inside the speed limit, I can keep up, and if he doesn't, then—'So long, pardner.' Seems kind of silly sticking together, though. The way roads are marked, nobody gets lost nowadays."

"But we're having lunch together," Ted reminded him, "and maybe I can persuade him to stop in and talk to Mr. Dobson, when we reach Forestdale."

"You going to suggest it?"

"Not till we get to Forestdale, and I see how time's running, and whether he has any other appointments. But even if it doesn't turn out that way, you make it more likely that he'll think of you in case something important turns up, when you leave the door open."

The first part of their drive was uneventful. It was a clear, cold day, and traffic was light. Mr. Prentice drove steadily, and well within the speed limits. Shortly after noon he signaled that he wanted to stop for lunch, and they nodded agreement. He turned in at a neat little roadside place, and alighting from the car, waited for them.

"Ted, I'm asking you in advance so as not to embarrass you: is it all right for me to buy your lunch?"

"Thanks," said Ted gratefully, "but Mr. Dobson wouldn't like it."

They had a pleasant lunch. Mr. Prentice proved to be an interesting talker. Without mentioning either the threatened strike or the court hearing, he entertained them with a few sidelights on a career that was strange to them.

"I don't know whether he's right or wrong," Nelson remarked as they took to the road again, "but I'm sure that he *believes* what he says is right. He's a sincere man."

"But that's not always a compliment—he could be sincere and still be stupid," Ted pointed out.

"Maybe—but Mr. Prentice is no stupe, either."

After passing through a little town called Echo, they found themselves on the wide, open road again. Mr. Prentice was some five hundred yards ahead of them, sweeping around a long, gentle curve. Suddenly a speeding car shot past them. The driver did not pull over to the side after passing them, but straddled the center line, apparently determined to pass Mr. Prentice's car as well. Nelson was concentrating on negotiating the curve, and Ted's eye was also off the other cars for a moment, so that neither actually saw what happened. All they observed was that the speeding car had gone on without pausing, and that Mr. Prentice's car had run off the road, plunged down the hill, turned over once, and landed on its side.

Nelson drew to a stop, and without speaking, the boys jumped out and ran down the hill. The doors on the topside remained closed, and Mr. Prentice apparently had made no effort to get out. They tried the handles, but either the doors were locked from the inside, or else the crash had jammed them. Nelson shaded his eyes and stared through the windowpane.

"I can see him moving," he announced. "The crash threw him over into the next seat, but he doesn't seem to be pinned or anything."

"Can he open the door?"

"I don't know. He's sort of threshing around as though he doesn't quite know what he's doing. Wait a minute. He sees me now."

In pantomime, Nelson motioned to Mr. Prentice to open the door. Ted was also looking inside now, through the back-seat window. Making an obvious effort, Mr. Prentice managed to boost himself to a raised position and tried the door, but it refused to open. Then Nelson motioned for him to try the rear door, which he did, with the same result. Apparently he was able to follow suggestions, though he still wasn't thinking too clearly on his own.

"What'll we do, get help?" asked Ted.

"How long will that take? Besides, what can they do except raise the car, and from the looks of it the other side is damaged worse than this. They'll have to end up cutting him out. No, I think the best thing to do is break in this back window."

"It'll be tough. This is safety glass, and it isn't even cracked."

"Lucky thing for him. There's nothing much worse than flying glass. Too bad this isn't one of those kick-out windows, though. Hunt up a couple of rocks, and I'll try to make him understand what we're doing."

By the time Ted returned, Nelson had made their intention known, and Mr. Prentice, having nodded his approval, was protecting himself as well as he could from the possibility of scattering glass. They were able to knock out a section of glass sufficiently large for Nelson to reach the wind-up handle. Carefully protecting his wrist from cuts, he was able to roll the window down a little, and through the larger opening at the top he could now reach the handle again, and roll the window down all the way. He was still unable to open the door, however, even from the inside.

If he were to get out very soon, Mr. Prentice would have to crawl through that open window. Fortunately, his mind now seemed a little clearer, and he was able to maneuver his head and shoulders through the opening. Then the boys were able to grab a shoulder each and give him some help. He was soon standing beside them, still a little dazed, but able to talk.

"I guess I was pretty lucky," he decided.

"Lucky!" Nelson exclaimed. "It looked to me as if that guy rode you right off the road on purpose."

"What for? What would he have against me?"

"How about something to do with the union," Ted suggested, "the strike or the court hearing?"

Mr. Prentice shook his head. "No, I can't see it. I'm not doing anything about calling a strike. I might even be able to head off a strike where another man couldn't. As for the court hearing, I can tell you in advance that I don't have any deep, dark secrets that are likely to hurt anybody. I'm simply going to tell the truth, and people can believe me or not."

"Then you think it was simply an accident?" asked Ted.

"Must have been. You meet a lot of those reckless characters on the road. I didn't see him in my mirror, but I did see another car coming from the opposite direction. Maybe he didn't see it in time, or thought he could make it past me. Then he had to cut in in front of me to get out of the way. And naturally he didn't stop afterward—that kind never does. Well, accident or on purpose, the result was just about the same either way."

"Well, where do we go from here?" asked Nelson restlessly.

Mr. Prentice stared at the car a moment. "It'll take a garage to handle that, all right. And I suppose we have to make some sort of report to the police. Echo's the nearest place. I imagine they'll have some kind of county or state police official there. If not, at least they'll have a telephone."

"How about a doctor?" asked Ted with some concern, for Mr. Prentice still wasn't looking too sharp.

"Oh, I guess I'll be all right. Still, I suppose a doctor would be the proper thing, in case the question of insurance liability came up—in fact, the police would probably insist upon it."

"Then let's find a doctor first," Ted suggested, "and he can tell us how to locate the police."

"If we climb up over this way, the hill isn't so steep, and I can bring the car around," Nelson offered. "Then it's back to Echo. I had a feeling that I hadn't seen the last of that burg."

CHAPTER 4

ECHO

DESPITE ITS SMALL SIZE, ECHO HAD A COMMUnity hospital, toward which Nelson was directed. Now that the first shock was wearing off, Mr. Prentice admitted to feeling some bruises. As Ted and Nelson waited in the corridor, he was given an emergency examination. Then he came out into the corridor to tell them the results.

"Nothing broken, but the doctor wants me to stay overnight as a precautionary measure. That seems overly cautious to me, but of course it's their job to be careful. He's telephoning the sheriff's office right now, and they'll probably send a man out. Don't leave until you've talked to him, since he'll want to get your account of the accident, too."

"Anything we can do, about the car or anything else?" Ted volunteered.

"No, Ted, I don't think so. There's a garage here in Echo, and I'll telephone while I'm waiting and make the necessary arrangements. And I'll have to cancel my appointment with my attorney in Forestdale. He's Mr. Waring. Do you know him?"

The boys nodded.

"He wanted to go over my testimony for the hearing tomorrow, but I guess we probably won't make it now. That's all right by me. I surely haven't anything to hide. I just hope the whole truth comes out. By the way, Ted, is it all right for me to give him your name, just in case he should want more information about the accident, or anything else you might be able to help with?"

"Of course, Mr. Prentice. I just wish we could do something more for you. It doesn't seem right to leave you here alone in the hospital."

"Nonsense. I owe you boys a great deal already, and don't think I don't appreciate it."

Fortunately he knew better than to offer them a reward, and so saved the boys the embarrassment of refusing. While Mr. Prentice made his calls, Ted, in another phone booth, called the *Town Crier* office, explaining the delay. Once he was certain neither of the boys was injured, Mr. Dobson asked them to stay in Echo as long as they could help Mr. Prentice.

When the policeman arrived on a motorcycle, Mr. Prentice was being formally admitted to the hospital, so the officer spoke with the boys first. Ted really had very little to tell, having seen nothing until the car had already left the road. Nelson's account was a little more complete. He knew the color of the other car, and thought he knew the make, but admitted he wasn't positive about it. He didn't have the license number, of course. And though Nelson made it clear that the other car was at fault, he said nothing to indicate that the incident had been deliberate. Ted had already advised him it would be better not to make any wild charges he couldn't support. Anyway, leaving the scene of an accident was already a serious enough charge.

The boys would have liked to see Mr. Prentice once more before leaving, but the officer was with him now, and a hospital attendant told them the patient could have no more visitors until evening. Rather reluctantly they set out for Forestdale.

"I didn't see much sense at first in the two cars sticking together," Nelson remarked, "but this time it was pretty useful—like the buddy system at camp."

"You still think it was done deliberately?" Ted inquired.

Nelson nodded. "All I can tell you is what I saw, and that's the way it looked to me. What about you, Ted?"

"I might believe it if I could see any sense to it. I don't see how it accomplished anything."

"Oh, a man like Mr. Prentice must have dozens of enemies. And if this was one of them, he played it mighty rough. You knew he was going to Forestdale, so I suppose other people could have known it, too."

"Yes, I expect so. It was mentioned in the paper that he had an appointment in Stanton Thursday morning, and of course he had a court hearing in Forestdale Friday morning, so the time he would be making the trip could be pinned down quite accurately. But if it were deliberate, do you think the car could have followed us all the way from Stanton?"

"No, I don't. Traffic was pretty light, and I could often see long, empty stretches back of me. I think that car must have picked us up in Echo."

* * * *

At the office a dozen odd jobs awaited Ted, and Nelson was also given a few errands which kept him hopping. Mr. Dobson and Miss Monroe had further questions about the accident, which Ted readily answered.

"You think he'll be able to get to the hearing tomorrow morning?" asked the editor.

"He said he would, and the doctor seemed to think so, too."

"How'd you like to cover the hearing for the paper, Ted?" inquired Mr. Dobson suddenly.

Ted was hardly surprised, but very much pleased. "Fine! But I thought you'd want to handle it yourself, Mr. Dobson."

"I did plan on it, but I find a number of different things have come up, and it'll be better for me to be here at the office where I can keep my finger on them. You needn't report here in the morning, but if you should find a break around the middle of the morning, call in. I'd like to be posted on how things are going."

Although Mr. Dobson undoubtedly was busy, Ted knew he must have had confidence in Ted's judgment or else he would have arranged to get there himself. So, for Ted, the working day ended on a happy note, in spite of their troubles. Nelson, too, admitted he was satisfied with his day's work.

"If Mr. Prentice had been alone, he might have been trapped there for hours before someone found him. I'm glad we could help him."

Because of the pressure of their holiday schedule, Ted was obliged to take some work home from the office with him. He sat down to it soon after supper, but had not proceeded very far before the telephone rang.

"Ted, this is Mr. Waring, Mr. Prentice's attorney."

"Yes, Mr. Waring. Mr. Prentice told me you might call."

"I've just had a long talk with Mr. Prentice by telephone, and I've had some bad news."

"Is he worse?" asked Ted anxiously.

"Oh, no, he's all right—physically. But that accident has put us in a bad hole, and he's worried about it. Did he tell you that he was carrying a microfilm of union records?"

"Well, yes, I think he did mention it," Ted recollected.

"Do you happen to know where he carried it?"

"No, he didn't say."

"It was in the door pocket—the door opposite the driver's seat. Later he checked with the garage, and they couldn't find it. He thinks it must have been thrown out of the car."

"I thought the doors were jammed shut."

"Apparently not. He thinks the right-hand door was sprung open as the car careened over, but that it finally landed on that side and jammed the door shut again. Either that, or it fell out somehow when the garage was righting the car preparatory to towing it in. However it happened, it's gone, and we're in a jam. Without that film there won't be any point to the hearing tomorrow morning."

"It seems to me that the accident gives you a legitimate excuse," Ted offered. "Can't you get a postponement?"

"There've been a couple of postponements already. Even if the court allows it, it will make a bad impression on the public. They might get the idea he's afraid to testify. I've warned him against any more postponements."

Ted was silent. It seemed to him that if you needed a postponement, then you needed it, whether it was good public relations or not. He waited, but the lawyer was silent—with the kind of silence which precedes the asking of a favor, Ted thought. He decided to inquire:

"Can't the microfilm be replaced?"

"Not very easily, Ted. There was only the one copy. Of course we still have the union records, but getting them filmed over again will take days of work. You know, Ted, it's possible that that film is still out there at the scene of the accident, lying on the ground. Do you think you could take a run out there and look for it?"

"Tonight? It wouldn't be very easy to find it in the dark."

"I know it's a terrible imposition, Ted, but the matter is awfully important to us, and Mr. Prentice said he felt I could call on you for any tasks that might come up."

"I guess I could," Ted agreed slowly. "Are you coming, too?"

"I wish I could, Ted, but I don't think I would be of much help in finding the film, and I've got several important things that have to be done before the hearing. You're almost the only one I can ask, since you're familiar with the accident scene. You can borrow my car if you want to."

"Thanks, but I can ask the friend I was with this afternoon. If he can't make it, I'll stop by for your car. Are you at your office?"

"Yes, and I'll be here till past midnight. Well, thanks a lot, Ted. Mr. Prentice and I both appreciate this very much. Call me when you get back, will you?"

"All right, I will. Good-by, Mr. Waring."

"Good-by, Ted. Good luck."

Nelson was agreeable to the trip, and provided them with some strong flashlights as well.

"But that place is beginning to haunt me," he admitted as they started out. "I've got a feeling that I'm going to spend the rest of my life just going to and from Echo."

At the scene of the accident, Nelson drew his car well off the road, and left the lights on. Though the wreck had been removed, they remembered the spot very distinctly, and explored the hillside as carefully as they could, following the course the car had taken, until they came to the place where it had stopped. The ground was frozen hard, but the trampling of the weeds showed where the garage men had been at work, and the course they had followed in towing out the car. But though the boys flashed their lights about in a wide circle, they were unable to find anything that resembled a roll of microfilm.

"The worst of it is," Nelson decided, "that it might be lying right out in plain sight, and we could easily find it in the daytime. These flashlights are all right, but they aren't the sun."

"You looking for the wreck?" a voice hailed them. "A car with a hook on it came and towed it away."

They turned their fights on the hill and saw a boy of about ten or eleven. He had a hockey stick flung over his shoulder, and ice skates dangled from it.

"How's the ice?" asked Nelson, deciding to try a friendly approach.

"Cold," said the boy. He came down the hill with no sign of timidity.

"We're looking for a small package which may have been lost out of the car," Ted explained.

"What did it look like?"

Ted made a vague motion with his hands. "I guess it was about this big—"

"Was it in a cardboard box?"

"Maybe it was, or maybe it fell out of the box."

"Probably in a tin container," Nelson spoke up. "Why, did you see a package?"

"No."

"What's your name?" Ted asked.

"Jerry Speck."

"Do you live in Echo?"

"No, I live in that house over there." They followed his nod, and could just see the roof of a house over the crest of the hill.

"Well, Jerry," Ted went on, "we're very anxious to find this package. Did you see anyone around who may have picked it up?"

"Nope. Just us guys who went skating, and the policeman, and the tow-truck men, and the scavenger."

"The scavenger!" Ted and Nelson exclaimed together.

"Yes."

"Who is he?" Ted questioned.

"He lives over that way, in a shack by the dump. Everybody says he's awfully rich. He's got a million dollars buried someplace."

"Was this scavenger here when nobody else was around?"

"Yes. He was looking around the car, and then we came and he went away. Then the policeman and the tow-truck men came. We saw them pull the car up the hill. That was when we were on our way home from the pond before supper."

"Well, Jerry, it's possible that the package is lying somewhere around here but we can't find it in the dark. How about you looking around in the morning to see if you can find it?"

"Is there a reward?" Jerry demanded.

"Reward? Oh, yes, I'm sure Mr. Waring would be glad to pay you a reward if you find it."

"Five dollars," said Nelson grandly, and added in an undertone to Ted, "It's not my money."

"Five dollars!" the boy exclaimed. "Sure, I'll look for it. What do I do if I find it?"

Ted took out his pencil and notebook. "Here's my telephone number. It's long distance, and you can call collect. I need it before nine o'clock."

Jerry took the paper excitedly and thrust it into his pocket as he ran off home.

"We're going to look up the scavenger, aren't we?" asked Nelson. Ted nodded and they started off in the direction Jerry had pointed out earlier.

"First time I ever heard one of those dump-pickers called a scavenger," Nelson observed. "I suppose it's the same thing as a beachcomber, except that he doesn't have a beach."

"Sure, and they've all got a million dollars buried somewhere," Ted remarked as they walked along. "He might not have the film, though. Maybe one of the boys picked it up."

"No, I don't think so. Not that I think all kids are honest, but they usually take something they want. Something like this they'd probably turn over to the police."

"Maybe not, if they were just curious to take it home and see what was inside."

"I suppose that's possible, but I don't think they could have done it without Jerry seeing them. That kid doesn't seem to miss much. And for five dollars he would surely have told us."

They reached the dump, which had a long dirt road leading up to it, and apparently was the main dump for villages for miles around. Most of the refuse had been plowed under and smoothed over with dirt on top, but they could see the uncovered part where recent dumping had taken place.

"Gee, maybe you could get rich at a job like this," Nelson speculated. "You always read stories about people accidentally throwing out their jewelry, and stuff like that. Maybe it's guys like this who find it."

"And, naturally, turn it back like honest people."

"Sure, sure they do—not! Well, where's that shack?"

They looked around in every direction, before finally spotting it. It was not far off, but was obscured by the shadow of nearby trees. The shack itself was entirely dark.

"Looks like nobody's home," Nelson decided.

"Unless he's sleeping. Well, let's try it, anyway. That's what we came for."

"Hope he doesn't have a shotgun," Nelson muttered. "If he really does have anything valuable, he's likely to be touchy about it."

At the front door they knocked loudly, then waited a minute or two, but there was no response from inside. Once more they pounded on the door, but there was still no answer.

"He couldn't be asleep after that," Nelson asserted. "He's either hiding, or else he's away. You know, this door isn't fastened very well. I bet I could break the lock in with about one good push."

"No, you don't." Ted laid a restraining hand on his arm. "You ever hear about burglary?"

"You mean breaking into this old shack would be burglary?" asked Nelson incredulously. "It's not like breaking into a house in town."

"Why isn't it? If somebody lives here, then it's his home. The law doesn't care how fine a home it is."

"I hate to go back without getting what we came for, though."

"We still have one chance," Ted pointed out as they started back toward the car. "Jerry may find it in the morning."

CHAPTER 5

OFF THE RECORD

TED WAITED AS LONG AS HE COULD IN THE morning for Jerry to call. Finally he was obliged to leave for the court room. Arriving there, he found things delayed a little, and called home, but his mother told him there had still been no word from Jerry. Ted hung up with a feeling of disappointment. It was a quarter after nine, and there was little chance of hearing from Jerry now.

"Well, I suppose he just didn't find it," Ted remarked to Nelson.

"Or maybe he didn't get a chance to look. What do you think this does to Mr. Prentice?"

"I don't know. It all depends on how Judge Harder looks at it. We ought to know that in a few minutes."

There was movement out in the corridor as a number of persons hurried to get into the room. Apparently word had been passed that the judge was about to enter. Among the latecomers was Mr. Prentice. He saw the boys, and gave them a hurried nod, but he was preoccupied with his attorney as they sat down at a table near the front. Ted noticed that the union official was limping a little and had a worried expression, but otherwise seemed all right.

Everyone rose as the judge entered, then seated themselves again and court was convened.

"Is the attorney for Mr. Prentice ready to produce the records which the court requested?" were the judge's opening words.

Mr. Waring stepped forward. "Your Honor, I am sorry to report that there has been a most unfortunate accident. While on his way to Forestdale yesterday, Mr. Prentice's car left the road, and he himself spent the night in a hospital. The microfilm on which the records had been transcribed disappeared from the car."

"I take it, then, that you do not have the records."

"Your Honor, it was completely unavoidable, and I assure you that we will make every effort to produce these records at the earliest possible time."

"Will Mr. Prentice please approach the bench?" The union official did so, and the judge continued, "You say that the microfilm disappeared from your car. Was there only one copy of this microfilm?"

"Yes, Your Honor. That is, I believe so. At least I know that *I* only had one copy."

"If there were another copy, who would have it?"

"Your Honor, I don't know of any other copy, but it occurs to me that the photographer may have some sort of negative from which he can easily print another copy."

"Did you make any effort to learn if this were so?"

"No, Your Honor. It did not occur to me until just this moment, but we could not have had it here in time for this morning's hearing anyway."

"Suppose there is no copy, what about the records themselves? Could not they be brought in?"

"I suppose they could, Your Honor, though a microfilm would make a much more effective presentation, since it could be viewed by all parties at once. However, the records are now scattered. The photographer was given instructions to dispatch them to the various local offices, and they are probably all in the mail at the present time."

"Well, I can see that everything appears to be against us as far as getting these records into court is concerned. Do you think you could have them in court by Tuesday morning?"

"I will certainly try, Your Honor. However, if there is no copy, we must get the records all together again, and get the photographer to work over the holidays. I can only try."

"Don't *try*, Mr. Prentice. *Do* it. There have already been far too many delays in these proceedings, and this court will allow no further delays except under the most urgent circumstances. Court is adjourned until Tuesday morning at nine o'clock."

They rose as the judge left the courtroom. Ted felt that once more things had fizzled out on him, and any chance of writing a good story for the *Town Crier* had now disappeared. By Tuesday morning he would be on his way back to college, and if Carl Allison wasn't back by that time, Mr. Dobson would have to cover the proceedings himself.

Since Mr. Prentice seemed busy, they started to leave without talking to him, but he caught Ted's eye, and motioned to them to wait. They did, and in a few minutes he joined them. Ted noticed that he was carrying a copy of that morning's *Town Crier.*

"Were you satisfied with my story, Mr. Prentice?" Ted inquired.

"Yes, Ted, I think you did a competent, unbiased job. Naturally, I would prefer to have the newspapers on my side, but it would be unreasonable to expect that. This interview with Mr. Abbott, however—do you think it's accurate?"

"Must be," Ted affirmed. "Mr. Dobson's very careful."

Mr. Prentice shook his head. "I'm sorry about that. If Mr. Abbott really believes all the things he says, I'm afraid we're in for trouble. He appears to be taking a stand from which it will be impossible for him to budge. Strangely enough, I have not yet met him, though I suppose I will soon. I'd like to see the sort of person he really is."

Then he turned to Nelson.

"I don't know much about these photography processes myself, but I realized at lunch yesterday you were a bug on the subject. Do you think the photographer would have a copy of that film?"

Nelson shook his head. "I doubt it."

"But when you print pictures, don't you have a negative, or something like that?"

"Yes, but that's different. I haven't seen this microfilm, but I imagine it's like movie film. That is, they are both positives—just the opposite of negatives. On expensive movies, they first make a negative, and then print a positive from that. But there's also a less expensive process which makes the positive directly without a negative. I should think that in microfilming they would use the cheaper direct process, since they wouldn't need the high-quality delineation."

Mr. Prentice groaned. "Well, I surely hope you're wrong, because if you're not, I'm due for the granddaddy of all headaches this weekend—and it won't be from celebrating the New Year. I guess I'd better get on the telephone and start the wheels turning. You don't suppose there's still any slight chance of finding that old film, do you?"

"We had a boy out there who promised to look this morning," Ted informed him, "but apparently he didn't find it."

"But he may not have been reliable," Nelson added quickly. "Want to go out for another look this afternoon, Ted?"

"I don't like to ask you fellows to do anything more for me," Mr. Prentice put in, "but it would surely help me out of a hole if you could find it. I can't go myself, because if things move as I expect, I'll have to leave town in the other direction immediately after lunch I hate to think it may still be lying out there on the ground, perhaps hidden in the weeds. I'd make it right with you if you wanted to look again."

"You've made it all right already," Ted assured him. "You gave me the interview I needed, so I'm more than glad to do something for you if I can. Maybe I could get off a little early this afternoon while there is still daylight."

"What color was the container?" asked Nelson.

"Orange. It's a cylinder box about this size." He gestured with his hands.

"What about that scavenger?" Ted inquired. "We could look him up again. He just might have picked it up."

"You mean that man you mentioned on the phone to Mr. Waring last night, Ted? I don't think he would have picked it up. Those men know what things have a salvage value. The film wouldn't have done him any good."

"Unless he thought there might be a reward for returning it," Nelson speculated.

"Well, yes, that's a possibility, of course, though it doesn't sound quite like the salvage men I've known. They appear to dislike getting involved with the police, as they well might over a matter like this. They'd be more likely to let it lie there. Still, I'm not inclined to overlook any possibilities, and if you want to check with him it would certainly be all right with me."

"I offered the boy a reward of five dollars," Nelson remarked.

"That certainly sounds very reasonable. I'd be willing to go as high as a hundred dollars if I had to, but don't let your scavenger know that. He might try to raise the amount even higher if he got the idea this was really valuable."

Ted returned to the office and brought Mr. Dobson up to date.

"You say Mr. Prentice is leaving town right after lunch? I wonder if I could stage a little conference right here between him and Mr. Abbott. It might serve to clear the air."

Privately Ted doubted that the two men would come, or that it would do any good if they did. However, when he returned to the office an hour later after doing some errands, he was surprised to see Ken Kutler, of the North Ridge *News-Record,* just getting out of his car.

"Hi, Ted," Ken called to him.

"Well, what are you doing here? Going to work for a good paper?"

"Oh, the *News-Record* keeps me on its payroll until it can afford to raise its standards. I understand there's a peace conference going on here, and I've been assigned to cover it."

"Then Mr. Dobson did manage to get everybody together?"

"Oh, yes, Mr. Abbott and Mr. Prentice both agreed to come, and I was invited, too, since there isn't going to be any story—it's all off the record. I suppose Mr. Dobson feels that if they can just get together unofficially, everyone'll let down his hair and get to know each other better."

"Don't you think so?" asked Ted, catching the cynicism in Ken's voice.

"Oh, sure, they'll get to know each other—the way a dog and a cat do and keep right on fighting. I'm not very sold on these secret conferences. The main trouble with them is that you can't keep them secret. Instead of letting the press cover the story objectively, they pledge everyone to secrecy, and then afterward each side leaks out its own version of what happened."

"If that's how you feel about it, why did you bother coming?" Ted demanded.

"For two reasons. The first is that I may pick up background information that will be useful in case of further developments in the story."

"And the other reason?"

"My editor told me I had to," said Ken solemnly, and Ted smiled.

Mr. Prentice's car drove up just then, showing some of the effects of the recent accident, although the garage had done a rapid fix-up job on it. He maneuvered the car in toward the curb, a little farther down the street, then came up to join them. He nodded cordially to Ken, then turned to Ted.

"Bad news for me, Ted. The photographer *doesn't* have a copy of that film. Worse yet, he's dispatched all the records back to the offices. This was earlier in the week, but he didn't send them first class, so it's anybody's guess whether they'll all be delivered by tomorrow or not. If not, I'm out of luck till Tuesday, and even if they are delivered I'm going to have to do some scurrying around to offices hundreds of miles apart. I'm due for a real hectic weekend. So if you should be able to find that film, it would be a ton off my shoulders. Call Mr. Waring if you do. He'll be able to reach me."

Although Ken had not been present in court that morning, Ted could tell—or thought he could tell—that Ken already knew about the missing film.

"You're not going to be able to get the records together by Tuesday, are you?" said Ted to Mr. Prentice.

"I don't know, Ted. It doesn't really look like it, but at least I'm going to have to convince Judge Harder that I made every possible effort to do it."

Another car pulled up. "There's Mr. Abbott," Ted remarked. "We may as well go in."

After Mr. Abbott came in, introductions were performed, but Mr. Abbott and Mr. Prentice gave each other only the briefest handshakes and Ted felt the electricity in the air as the conference was about to begin.

CHAPTER 6

A PEACE CONFERENCE

"TO BEGIN WITH," MR. DOBSON OPENED WITH special courtesy toward the elder of his guests, "suppose you tell us, Mr. Abbott, what the issues are in this matter, as you see them."

"I think that's very clear," said the trucking owner, with a crispness which made no effort to conceal the bitterness lying beneath. "The issue is that the trucking companies are the victims of a slow-down strike. I don't want a strike any more than anyone else, but at least a strike would be fairer, and it would show the public just where the trouble was sprouting from."

"Let's try to stick to this one point for the moment," Mr. Dobson suggested. "How would you answer that charge, Mr. Prentice?"

"I'd answer it by saying that it isn't happening. I deny that the absentee rate is exceptionally high for the winter season, and while there have been a series of accidents, those things often run in cycles. Now I'm going to be frank and say there is a small grain of truth in what Mr. Abbott says. It's true that we have a small handful of trouble-makers in the union. We have to crack down on them once in a while, and we can do it if we're allowed to."

"You admit you can't always control your own men?" asked Mr. Abbott. "Then how can you expect the owners to deal with you as though you were a responsible organization?"

"Who controls the hiring in this industry?" Mr. Prentice retorted. "It's the companies that hire the men, and then our contract forces us to accept them as union members. We don't want them any more than the companies want them, but we're stuck with them. I sometimes think the companies deliberately hire these trouble-makers in order to embarrass the union."

"That's ridiculous, of course," said Mr. Abbott witheringly. "I'm sure that the companies always hire the best men that are available to them. What purpose would they have in hiring incompetent workers?"

"Maybe the company's standard of competency isn't the same as the union's. It might find that an unskilled driver with a background of anti-unionism would be a very satisfactory employee."

"May I point out to you, Mr. Prentice, that although it is true that the companies hire the workers, it is the union that won't let us fire them after they have shown themselves to be incompetent. If the employers occasionally make a mistake, it is the union that prevents them from correcting the error."

"Supposing we did let you fire anyone you wanted to, then what would happen to our seniority rights? We do let you fire anyone that has proved incompetent. All we ask is that you show justifiable cause."

They were obviously not going to settle that issue, nor any of the other points they discussed rather bitterly.

Ted thought that Ken was looking slightly amused, as though everything was turning out just about the way he expected. Mr. Dobson took charge once more.

"I don't think it's necessary for us to attempt to decide *all* the differences between management and labor here. But there does seem to be a fundamental difference of opinion on the facts of this case. What would you say, Mr. Abbott, if an impartial citizens' committee were appointed to determine just what is going on?"

"I'd say, Mr. Dobson, that while I ordinarily would not hold out against such a step, I think in this case it is unnecessary, or at least premature. We already have a court doing that for us. Though the union has done everything possible to delay proceedings, I don't think Judge Harder will stand for much more of it. By that time we will be able to determine whether the union leaders are the type of men that it is possible to deal with on an honorable basis."

He rose and turned his back on Mr. Prentice. "I'm a busy man, and I don't think there is much point in continuing this discussion. I only came because I didn't want it to appear that management was holding out against negotiations. But I do appreciate your efforts, Mr. Dobson. Good morning, everyone."

He put on his hat, buttoned his coat, and left the office. Mr. Prentice managed a little laugh, though it was easy to see how much he had been hurt by Mr. Abbott's attack.

"I suppose I ought to blow my stack, but much as I feel like it, I realize that wouldn't accomplish anything for the union. Well, I think I'd better be on my way, too. It was nice meeting you, Mr. Dobson, and Miss Monroe. Good day, gentlemen of the fourth estate." He nodded toward Ken and Ted, and left.

"Well, Ken, I'm sorry I brought you over here for nothing," Mr. Dobson apologized.

"Oh, that's all right, Mr. Dobson. I enjoy a good scrap, as long as I'm not in it."

After Ken had gone, Ted asked his editor: "Which one did you think was more nearly right, Mr. Dobson—Mr. Abbott or Mr. Prentice?"

"How can you say either one is right, Ted? They have each taken a stand which can lead only to bad results if they stick to it. When two men are paddling the same canoe, it isn't necessary for them to like each other, but at least they have to agree on where they're going, or they end up going nowhere at all."

There was so much to do in the office that Ted hesitated to ask permission to get off early. But finally, as four o'clock arrived and the work seemed to be getting under control, he broached the matter to the editor.

"I don't have to go if you need me, Mr. Dobson. We did promise, but maybe Nelson could handle it all right alone."

"Oh, that's all right, Ted. I think we're pretty well caught up here, and I'd rather you went along with Nelson as the paper's representative. Finding that piece of film could be very important. Who knows, there may be a story in it yet."

Nelson arrived before four-thirty, and the boys set off. The sky was overcast, but they hoped to have enough daylight left to make a thorough search. Nelson parked the car on the same spot as the previous night, and once more they scoured the hillside without result.

"At least we know what sort of box we're looking for," Nelson stated, "and that's more than we knew last night."

"If it's still in the container," said Ted cautiously. "The box might have come open, you know."

"Sure, but then at least we ought to find the container."

At the spot where the wrecked car had come to a stop, they searched with special care in an ever-widening circle, but with no luck. At last, with the light failing, they decided to give up.

"What do you think?" asked Ted. "Is there any chance it's here but we just haven't found it?"

"I don't know," said Nelson. "You know, it could be. There're all these little clumps of weeds about. We *ought* to be able to see it, but if it was hidden just right, maybe not. I don't *think* it's here, but I wouldn't stake my reputation on it. Anyway, I'll bet Jerry gave this place a pretty thorough going-over this morning, and he didn't find it either."

"There's still a little daylight left. Do you suppose we should check to see if it dropped out of the car while they were towing it away?"

"It doesn't sound likely, and anyway, even if it did, you don't expect to search all the way from here to Echo, do you? Besides, what about the scavenger? If we're going to interview him, I'd just as soon have a little daylight working on my side. Not that I'm scared—much. I'm just cautious."

"Maybe the scavenger would be a better bet. But that isn't saying he'd tell us, even if he did have it."

"Look for shifty eyes. That'll usually tell you if he's lying or not."

It was almost completely dark by the time they arrived at the scavenger's hut. This time they were a little luckier, however, for there was a light on. There was also a small delivery truck parked nearby, which they hadn't observed on the previous occasion. Ted knocked on the door.

"Who's there?" came the answer from within.

"Somebody to see you," Ted responded. It was a rather silly answer, but he hardly knew what else to say. Their names would have been meaningless to him, and Ted thought that identifying himself as a newspaper reporter might only scare him.

Anyway, the answer was enough to get the scavenger to open the door. He barred the way, however, and with the light behind him he was in a better position to study them than they were him.

"What do you want?" he asked.

"My name is Ted Wilford, and this is my friend, Nelson Morgan. May we come in and talk to you for a few minutes?"

He studied them for a moment longer, and then apparently decided they were harmless.

"Come on," he invited, stepping out of their way, "though it's not the Eden Park."

Inside the shack they found there was only one chair, besides a very beat-up old bed, and they decided they would rather stand. They turned to get a better look at their somewhat reluctant host.

The first surprise was his age. They had somehow expected him to be a very old man, instead of middle-aged. Though he had not shaved for a couple of days, his hair was neatly trimmed, and he seemed to have made some effort to clean himself up after his day's work. This clearly wasn't an old man who had "gone to seed," but instead a younger man who had apparently found a good business for himself.

Ted came directly to the point. "Did you know there was an auto wreck off the hill yesterday afternoon?"

The man nodded. "One of the dump-truck men told me about it."

"Well, there was something missing from the car. A little roll of microfilm. It wouldn't be of any value to you, but the driver is anxious to get it back. Did you find it?"

For answer the man reached up to a shelf. "Is this what you want?" he asked, handing them a small orange cylinder.

CHAPTER 7

THE SCAVENGER'S REPORT

TED FOUND HIMSELF BREATHING EASIER. HE had long ago given up hope of recovering the film, but it was pleasant to be proved wrong.

"I guess that's it," he said, and looked it over briefly before he handed it to Nelson. The package appeared to be sealed, just as it had come from the photographer's, so they did not open it, but Nelson shook it to satisfy himself that the film was inside.

"Where did you find it?" he asked. "By the car?"

"Technically, no, but near the spot where the car had been. The car was gone by the time I reached the place, and so I easily spotted the orange container. I picked it up and put it in my pocket, intending to turn it over to the police at the first chance. I would probably have driven in to the station later today, if you hadn't come along. There didn't seem to be anything very urgent or valuable about it. It's just a roll of movie film, isn't it?"

"Well, no," Ted explained. "It's a microfilm of some business records. It's important to the man who lost it, but you're right—it wouldn't be valuable to anyone else. I might be able to arrange a little reward for you, however."

"Oh, don't bother." The scavenger waved his arm, as though the thought annoyed him. "I don't think I deserve anything just for picking it up, the way anyone would have done who happened along."

"It's all right by us," Nelson agreed. "I wish we could have found this last night, though. We would have saved this man a peck of trouble. We came out here, but you weren't home."

The scavenger raised his brows. "Is that so? I'm sorry, but I was gone on business last night—but nowhere near the police station, I might add. Still, if that's the case, perhaps it would have been better if I had left it lying on the ground."

"Oh, no," Ted assured him. "Perhaps someone else would have picked it up, and anyway we might not have been able to find it in the dark. We're really very grateful to you."

After thanking the scavenger once more, the boys left. A light snowfall was beginning as they headed back toward the car, and they turned up their collars.

"That was a surprise, wasn't it?" Nelson remarked. "I wonder why he returned it? He could just as easily have discarded it some-where, and denied ever being near the place. That was one lie he told us, wasn't it, Ted?"

"Yes, I guess so. Jerry said he saw him while the car was still there, and he said he arrived after the car was gone. Of course, I sup-pose it's possible he was there twice."

"No dice, Ted. He took what he wanted the *first* time, when he gave that car a going-over. Of course he wanted to deny that he had ever been near the car, so he said he'd found it on the ground. I can't understand why he returned the film at all."

"He had to, Nel, as soon as he knew it was something that might be so valuable the police would make a stew over it. I think Mr. Pren-tice was right—his kind doesn't like to get mixed up with the police. Maybe there are a few things going on there that he doesn't want them to nose into. But there was another lie. He never had any inten-tion of turning this film over to the police. If someone came looking for it he figured it might be safer to give it up. But if no one did, then he'd simply forget about it."

"I think I spotted another lie, too," said Nelson slowly.

"You mean about being away last night?"

"No, I believe that, all right. His truck was gone, you know. But I think he was lying about not knowing what kind of film was in that package. Look, we know he went over the car. He was searching for anything that might be valuable to him. Most of the stuff wouldn't do him any good, so he let it alone. Then he saw this orange can. He didn't have a chance to examine it, so he simply put it in his pocket and ducked away. Now what would you do when you got home with a strange package? At the very least you'd read the label, wouldn't you? After all, it might be a stick of dynamite, for all you knew. And he wouldn't have had to read very far on this label before he knew what it was."

"But he didn't open it, and he didn't seem interested in a reward."

"I know. He was pretty forceful about that. Do you think he expected us to argue him into accepting a reward?"

"No, I don't," said Ted, puzzled. "He acted uneasy, as though the idea of a reward sort of scared him. I suppose it was the thought that he might have taken something valuable. Otherwise, who would be scared about being offered a reward?"

"Well, there were three lies, anyway—pretty good for such a short conversation. Do you figure we owe Jerry anything? He was pretty set on that five-dollar reward, and even though he didn't actually find the film, he did tell us about the scavenger."

"I don't know. I suppose that would be up to Mr. Prentice."

"Sure, but don't you think we at least ought to let him know we found the film? People wouldn't think it was right to let an *adult* waste his time hunting for something that wasn't there, but it's all right if a little kid does it."

"O.K., you convinced me." Ted smiled. "We'll go and see Jerry."

They found Jerry and his parents at home and Nelson showed Jerry the box of film.

"Oh, you found it?" said Jerry in disappointment.

"Well, you helped us find it, Jerry," Nelson explained. "It was the scavenger who picked it up, and he returned it to us. We wouldn't have known about him if you hadn't told us."

"Then who gets the five dollars?" Jerry demanded. "Is it the scavenger? He doesn't need it. He's got a million dollars buried."

"That was all Jerry could talk about last night," said Mrs. Speck with a smile. "I ought to explain that Jerry is saving up for a new bicycle. We thought he would appreciate it more if he earned the money himself."

"But giving directions to strangers isn't the type of work we had in mind," Mr. Speck added. "Out here in the country we just call that being neighborly. That's why we couldn't let him accept the reward in any case. No short cuts," he added warningly to his son. "You have to work for it."

"But he did spend some time looking for the package," Nelson pointed out. "That was work, wasn't it?"

"How long did you spend looking for the package, Jerry?" his father asked him.

" 'Bout an hour." His father looked at him sharply, and he looked down at the floor. "Maybe it was only forty-five minutes."

"You'll let me pay him for that, won't you?" asked Ted, taking out his wallet.

"Well—no more than a dollar, then. That's plenty," Mr. Speck decided.

Jerry accepted the dollar with glee, for a dollar bill evidently meant more to him than the promise of five dollars.

"That scavenger has a pretty good thing going for himself," Nelson remarked on the way home. "I wouldn't mind doing work like that for a while—I mean, if it's honest, and if I didn't have any family to support. I'd make my pile, and blow it all for a trip around the world."

"With your camera, of course."

"Why, certainly with my camera. What would be the use of traveling otherwise? I imagine that scavenger has a pile put away—maybe not a million dollars, but at least a . . . Ouch!" he exclaimed suddenly.

"What's the matter?"

"Oh, don't pay any attention to me. I just had one of my stupid ideas."

"Well, why don't you go ahead and tell me," said Ted patiently, "and save me the trouble of coaxing it out of you?"

"Look, I've had a lot of stupid ideas in my life, but this one is really stupid, even for *me*." He paused to choose his words carefully. "I was just wondering if this is really the microfilm we're looking for."

"What do you mean?" exclaimed Ted, amazed. "How could it be a different one? There couldn't have been *two* of them lost and found, could there? And the box isn't even opened, so it doesn't look like anybody tampered with it."

"I know, I know. I told you it was a stupid idea. Forget it."

They drove on in silence for a few minutes. Finally Ted groaned.

"What's the matter now?" asked Nelson. "It *was* a dumb idea, wasn't it?"

"Sure, it was," Ted agreed. "Of all the screwball ideas I ever heard of, that one is the very dumbest of them all."

"You think there might be something in it?" asked Nelson, brightening.

"No, I don't. I think it's the most ridiculous, nonsensical idea I ever heard of. It just doesn't make any kind of sense at all. Just the same it's something we've got to think about."

"Why think about it? It's something we can easily check, isn't it?"

"Can we?"

"Sure, why not? We could rent a projector from a photographer and look it over. Or does that sound wrong to you—like reading someone else's diary?"

"No, I don't think it would be wrong. It's something that's going to be made public in court anyway. And Mr. Prentice asked us to find the film and return it to him, so I don't see that we're doing any harm by checking to make sure it's the right one. What I'm wondering is, how would we know whether it's the right one?"

"Well, we could see if it carries the union records at least, couldn't we?"

"Yes, I suppose we could do that. Oh, I'm all for it. The way everything happened *was* sort of queer, wasn't it, though?"

"Yes, it was queer. Ted," Nelson went on soberly, "you're not thinking the same thing I am, are you?"

"I surely wish I wasn't. You mean about Mr. Prentice, don't you? You're wondering if he's everything he seems to be?"

"That's it, Ted. But how could it be different from the way it appears? You don't think Mr. Prentice deliberately wrecked his own car, do you? That's the hard way to lose a microfilm, if that's what he wanted to do."

"Well, maybe it *was* an accident, but maybe he *did* want to lose the microfilm all the same. He may even have wanted us along as witnesses to how it was lost. Then the accident came—"

"He couldn't have planned to lose it after that accident, Ted. He really was dazed—or else he deserves the Academy Award for acting."

"Yes, I agree on that. But at the hospital he could have phoned the scavenger—"

"He wouldn't have a telephone in that old shack, would he?"

"No, I guess not. I mean that Mr. Prentice might have had some way of getting the message to him. He wanted to get the scavenger to pick up that film."

"Then why did the scavenger give it back to us, Ted?"

"Yes, that still doesn't make much sense, does it—unless this isn't the same film."

"For that matter, Ted, how do we know Mr. Prentice ever had the right film in his car at all?"

"You mean he might have had a different film with him? Or maybe he didn't have *any* film with him. The scavenger might have had it all along."

"Don't make my head swim that way, Ted. I won't be able to drive. As soon as you begin to suspect that somebody's trying to put something over on us, it offers a lot of possibilities, doesn't it?"

"Yes, but we'll be home soon, and we can check this film, and then try to figure out where we stand."

"All right, Ted, but I sure hope it's the right film. If not, we're out a dollar."

This forced Ted to laugh, for the dollar was certainly the least of their troubles. Nelson joined in when he got the point.

"Where to, Ted?" asked Nelson as they entered Forestdale.

"Grub first. Drop me off at my place. Or why don't you stay and have supper with me? Then we can go ahead with the projector afterward. I don't know how long it will take, but we've got all evening. My mother said she'd leave supper on the stove, and you can be pretty sure she left enough for two. She was probably half expecting you."

This prediction proved to be true, and Ted soon had their supper warmed and on the table. As they ate, they speculated further on the possibilities of this case in which they suddenly found themselves involved.

CHAPTER 8

HOT STUFF

AFTER SUPPER THE BOYS DROVE TO THE PHOtographer's shop. Having learned what they wanted, he asked to see the container, read the label, and brought out the right-sized projector and a matching screen. He gave a few explanations to Nelson, who quickly grasped its operation.

"Thanks. We'll have this back later this evening—I guess—if that's all right with you. Do you want a deposit for the rental?"

"Oh, I don't think that will be necessary," said the proprietor. "Just sign for it, and if you bring it back tonight in good shape, there won't be any rental for it. I use this projector for advertising purposes. I'm trying to get people interested in what can be done with microfilm."

Nelson signed the book, they thanked him once more, and left the store, carrying the case and the screen. Back at Ted's home, they set up the projector and screen in the living room, then turned out all the lights except a low-power night lamp.

"Let her roll," Nelson called.

Ted snapped the switch on the extension cord, and Nelson turned on the projector. At first it was badly out of focus, but he quickly adjusted it, and the picture came on the screen. Unlike a movie projector, this projector showed only one frame at a time, and the operator switched to the next frame whenever he was ready. The first picture told them very little. It was a noncommittal letter from someone they had never heard of to another stranger.

"Look, though," Ted observed. "That letter is on the union's letterhead. At least this must be the right film."

"Yes, I guess it is," Nelson agreed, managing to sound a little relieved and a little disappointed at the same time.

Other letters followed, equally innocuous as far as they could tell. Nelson began to feel impatient.

"Ted, do we have to read through all this dry-as-dust correspondence? It doesn't mean anything as far as I can tell, so what's the use of it? You really can get a big book down on a little film like this, can't you? If we try to read it all, it's going to take us all night."

"Well, let's go on a little further, anyway. This group of letters seems to be ending. Now what's next?"

"This looks like bookkeeping records. Do you know anything about bookkeeping, Ted?"

"All I know is that there are debits and credits, and if they don't come out even at the end of the month you fire your bookkeeper."

"Yes, that's about all I know, too, so I don't see that this section is going to do us any good. What do these records look like to you?"

"They seem to be records of dues collected and checks written. Well, maybe all this will mean something to the court, but it doesn't mean much to us. We don't know whether these checks are proper or not. Let's see what comes on after this."

Nelson flipped rapidly through the bookkeeping records. They had already been looking at the film for about twenty minutes, and still had seen only a small part of it. Then the columns of neat figures abruptly stopped, and a new series of letters appeared. Nelson stopped at the first of these. It seemed to be an innocent-enough letter, merely requesting an appointment, until Ted noticed the name at the bottom.

"Jed Myers! He's the racketeer all the fuss has been about. Then the union *did* have dealings with him!"

Nelson was growing more excited, too. "Now wait a minute, Ted. This doesn't mean anything so far. All he did was ask for an appointment. It's what happened *after* the appointment that counts. Let's see what else it's got."

He flipped to the next letter. Apparently this was written after the meeting, for it referred to the agreements reached there, and said that the percentages would be satisfactory.

"Wow!" Nelson exclaimed. "This looks serious, if it means what I think it means. How does it look to you, Ted?"

"I don't know—but I know how it's going to look to most people. It looks like the union made a deal with the racketeers to give them a certain percentage as 'protection.' See if there's anything more on there. So far all we've got are letters written by Jed Myers. What does the union have to say for itself?"

Nelson flipped to the next letter. This one was indeed written from the union to Jed Myers. It acknowledged and thanked him for his previous letter, and expressed satisfaction that they had been able to arrive at a mutually satisfactory agreement. Ted could not help but feel a little sick over it.

"Who's that man who signed that letter—Channing Noble?" Nelson questioned. "Have you ever heard of him?"

"Have I ever heard of him? Sure, I have. He was Mr. Prentice's rival for the post of executive secretary. I understand there was a pretty bitter battle over it before the election, but afterward everything was smoothed over."

"Well, then, that still doesn't prove anything against Mr. Prentice. If it was Channing Noble who made the deal, and he wasn't even an officer in the union—"

"Do you think something big like this could go on, and Mr. Prentice not know anything about it?" asked Ted bitterly. "Maybe it was better to have somebody handle the deal who *wasn't* a union officer, just in case something should ever come up about it. But don't kid yourself about that. If there really was such a deal, Mr. Prentice must have known about it, and must have approved of it."

"This has got me baffled, Ted. If all this is true, and there was a deal like this, why should they have put it down on paper where it might come to light? Why should these letters have been put on the microfilm, when it would have been such a simple matter to destroy them?"

"Maybe each side *wants* to keep letters like this, in order to hold something over the other side," Ted pointed out. "Or they may have gotten on the film by accident. The court told him to produce the correspondence and bookkeeping records covering a certain period. Maybe he told the branch offices to submit their records for that period, and they were turned over to the photographer without ever being sorted. Look how much space these records take even on a microfilm, and then think what a stack the original records must have made. No wonder Mr. Prentice was dubious about getting them recorded again before Tuesday."

"Then you think Mr. Prentice didn't know these letters were on the film?"

"That's the way it looks to me. Oh, don't forget that he intended to meet with his lawyer before the court hearing on Friday. I can bet you anything they were planning to run over this film to see if there was anything on it that might hurt them. If they did that, and discovered these letters, they could have cut them out of the film, couldn't they, and then spliced the remaining pieces together so that no one would know?"

"Yes, they could have done that, I suppose, except that if anybody looked at the film strip closely he would be able to tell that a splice was made. Wait a minute, though. There's something else they could have done. After they had the film spliced together again, they could have had another copy of it made, and then submitted this copy to the court. The copy would have the same information on it, but it wouldn't show a splice."

"Yes, I guess that was how they planned to do it," said Ted dully. "At least I'm almost certain they intended to look the film over first, and when they discovered these letters, what would they have done about it? Only an awfully honest person would take letters like these into court, when he could so easily snip them out with a scissors. Are you that honest? I'd like to think I am, but I'll never be sure until I'm put to the test sometime."

"Just the same, Ted, a court order isn't something that you disobey lightly. Maybe Mr. Prentice would be afraid *not* to take these letters into court. Maybe someone else has seen them and reported on them, which would really put him on the spot. Anyway, that's the way I'd look at it. Oh, I believe in obeying the law, because that was the way I was brought up. But I'm not sure I obey it because I'm honest, or because I'm chicken."

"The funny thing about it is that I'm *sure* Mr. Prentice is an honest man. I mean he is honest according to his own standards. But some people have peculiar standards. They feel if they are trying to do something important, as long as they accomplish it, it doesn't matter much *how* they do it. If Mr. Prentice thought he would help the union by cutting out those letters, maybe he'd think that was the right thing to do."

"There's another way of looking at it, too, Ted. You think maybe he planned to cut these letters out, but he *did not* cut them, after all—anyway not yet. How do you know he ever planned to do it? He may have known they were on that film all the time, and intended to leave them there. Oh, not just because he was being honest. Remember, Ted, those letters don't mention Mr. Prentice; they concern Mr. Noble, his rival. Maybe he figured this would be a good way of getting Mr. Noble out of the picture and giving himself a free hand in the union."

"You mean he would deliberately do something that would hurt the union, just to strengthen his own position? If so, he's just about the lowest kind of skunk."

"You can double that with onions. Wheels within wheels. Nothing's ever as simple as it looks, is it? But maybe we're being too harsh on Mr. Prentice, Ted. We aren't sure that he knows about these letters. We aren't sure that he will cut them out when he finds out about them. And even if he does cut them out, maybe he wants to help the union."

"What about the deal with Jed Myers? It's barely possible he doesn't know anything about it right now, but will after he studies this film. Then what will he do about it? Cutting out the letters would show that he was trying to cover it up, wouldn't it?"

"Maybe not, Ted. He might simply feel that open court isn't the best place to take care of the matter. Maybe he'd rather do it quietly, after the publicity has subsided."

"But meanwhile he's going to have to lie about it in court. That's something, isn't it?"

"Yes, I guess so." Nelson laughed. "It looks like Mr. Prentice has got himself in one of those spots where you can't win. If he covers up these letters, he's lying. If he doesn't cover them up, he may be trying to wreck the union to get rid of Mr. Noble. It'll be interesting to see which way he decides to play it. Are you going to tell him we've seen these letters?"

"Not me!" said Ted hastily. "I've found out that when I don't know what to say, the best thing is to keep my mouth shut."

"Well, then, that puts it up to Mr. Prentice. As long as he doesn't know we know about the letters, he can make his own choice. He can tell the box was opened, but that won't necessarily mean anything.

The scavenger may have opened it just to see what was in it. You *are* going to turn the film over to Mr. Prentice, aren't you, Ted?"

"Before I do anything," said Ted firmly, "I'm going to talk it over with Mr. Dobson. I earn my salary by doing what he tells me, and this is one time I'm glad to be told."

"You want to see anything more of this, Ted?" Nelson had flashed on a long series of pictures in rapid succession. It seemed to be another series of bookkeeping records which didn't mean anything to them.

"No, shut it off. I've had enough for tonight."

"O.K., then. I'll wind this up and return the projector to the photographer. But Ted, I'm beginning to think we've got hold of something that's really hot. I'd advise you not to let that roll out of your sight."

"Don't worry. I'm going to make sure all the doors and windows are locked tonight, and I'm going to sleep with it under my pillow. As far as I'm concerned, it's a real hot potato, and the sooner I can get it off my hands the better."

Having reversed the film, Nelson took it off the spool and replaced it in the container. He carefully handed it to Ted.

"Now don't forget I gave it to you," he cautioned with a laugh. "I'm not in this. All I did was offer to drive you down to Stanton for an interview, and right away I find myself up to my neck in trouble. Talk about bad companions! I wonder why my mother even lets me associate with you any more."

"Don't forget that renting this projector was *your* idea," Ted reminded him.

"That's right." Nelson admitted. "I must say it wasn't exactly a brain storm."

"Oh, what difference does it make? The letters are on the film. Suppose we didn't know about them? That wouldn't change the situation any, would it?"

"At least *we* wouldn't be in the middle of it—although as long as nobody knows we know about the letters, I suppose it doesn't matter much."

After packing up the projector and screen, Nelson left. Ted tried to settle down for the rest of the evening, but found his thoughts were troubled. He read the paper, watched part of a hockey game on TV, and finally took a shower. On hearing his mother come in quite late, he went downstairs to talk with her for a little while. She was happy about the party, and Ted did not tell her about his own problems with the film. Not yet, anyway, for he felt there was a decision coming up he would have to make himself. Before returning upstairs, he checked all the locks once more.

He slept restlessly, and awakened several times during the night. The presence of the film under his pillow was hardly comforting. He wished now he had never had anything to do with it.

CHAPTER 9

THE RIOT SCENE

AT THE OFFICE IN THE MORNING, TED TOLD MR. Dobson all about the microfilm. The editor listened carefully. When Ted was finished, Mr. Dobson finally said:

"Well, Ted, I don't see that we have very much choice in this matter. This is obviously Mr. Prentice's film, so we'll have to return it to him at the earliest possible moment. Remember that, so far, we aren't sure that Mr. Prentice has done anything wrong. He may, or he may not, know about those letters on the film. He was very anxious to get the film back, but we don't know whether that was because of the letters he knew were on it, or because he was merely trying to comply with the court order. Now if he presents the film to the court, with all the letters still on it, then I would say he still hasn't done anything wrong as far as the court hearing is concerned, though the deal with Mr. Myers is wrong."

"But what if he *doesn't* present the film with everything still on it?" Ted questioned anxiously. "Then how do I stand?"

Mr. Dobson continued to look serious. "This isn't anything I want to involve the newspaper in, Ted, and whether you should delay your return to college to offer your testimony in court must be a matter for your own conscience. If you had testimony that might prevent an innocent man from being convicted, then I would certainly think it was your duty to testify, but it isn't that sort of hearing. This is only a preliminary hearing, though of course it might lead to a criminal prosecution later. Suppose you did testify, just what could you testify to?"

"To the letters I saw on the film that Mr. Prentice afterward cut out."

"Now think this over carefully, Ted. If you were to testify to one thing, and Mr. Prentice to the opposite, it would be simply one man's word against another's. That isn't the best sort of evidence, and probably wouldn't help to prove anything at all. I have to tell you that there would be some prejudice against you because of your age, since young people are not considered entirely reliable in their testimony. I'm not even sure that the prosecuting attorney would want your report. He might see too many difficulties in the way."

"Nelson could back up my story. That would help, wouldn't it?"

"Yes, Ted, I suppose it would, though the fact that he is a close friend would count against you. But Mr. Prentice might have some close associates to back up his story. Let's continue for a minute. Exactly what could you testify to? Have you memorized those letters? No, certainly you haven't, and the exact wording, the dates, signatures, and all the other details might be very important. Without the actual signatures available, no handwriting analysis would be able to prove that the letters were authentic. And even if all these things weren't true, you still have never seen the original letters, don't know where they came from or how they got on the film, you can't account for every person who has handled the film, and so on."

"But haven't I got all the proof I need right here?" Ted patted his coat pocket in which he was carrying the film.

"But you won't even have that, Ted, when you've returned the film to Mr. Prentice."

"Couldn't I have those letters copied by the photographer before I return the film?"

"I don't know whether the photographer could and would do it for you, Ted. But photographing letters to which you have no right might put you on rather shaky legal ground. Altogether, Ted, I feel your testimony would be very ambiguous in any case, and there's no reason you should feel obliged to offer it. It's up to the prosecution to develop its own case. Of course if you were subpoenaed, it would be a different proposition."

Ted felt relieved, and showed it. "That's all right, then. I certainly wasn't anxious to testify, but I didn't want to get into any trouble over it, either. I'll just be glad to head back for college Tuesday morning, and I hope no one stops me first!"

He put through a call to Mr. Waring's office, but was told that the attorney would not be in until eleven o'clock. Even though he felt as if the film were burning a hole in his pocket, he decided it might be better to keep it until he could deliver it in person. This decision was reinforced by circumstances, for they were faced with a busy morning. But even his regular duties had to wait, as a telephone call came in.

"There's some strike rioting going on out on the old Post Haste Road, about a mile or two beyond town," Miss Monroe told them. "Some of the union men have stopped a cooperative milk truck trying to bring a shipment through into Forestdale without union drivers. It sounds pretty ugly, as though someone might get hurt."

"Who called?" Mr. Dobson asked.

"He didn't give his name. He sounded too excited for that."

"How about the police?" asked Ted.

"Apparently it's just outside the town limits, and it would take hours to get the sheriff's office on the job—even if they had the men to cope with a situation like this, which they don't. I suppose the strikers were careful not to get involved with the local police."

"No strike had been called up to nine o'clock," Mr. Dobson observed. "This must be a bunch of wild-catters trying to jump the gun. They often feel if they act on their own, they can force the union to back them up later. If so, they're making a mistake there. It helps rouse public resentment against them. Besides, Mr. Prentice isn't the sort of man who can be pushed into a decision against his will. I suppose you'd better get out there, Ted. Do the best you can with the story, but don't endanger yourself."

"How about pictures?" asked Ted excitedly. "I'll bet Nelson would give anything to have this chance, especially if he had a newspaper back of him."

"Yes, it might be a good idea to have Nelson along, Ted. Two of you would be better than one, and I might be able to use some pictures, too. Why don't you phone him, and Miss Monroe will have a press card filled out for him by the time he gets here."

Not only was Nelson willing to go, but he was very happy over his press card.

"I wish I could keep it, but I suppose Mr. Dobson will want it, after we get back to the office."

"*If* we get back to the office."

"Sounds really serious, huh, Ted?"

"Apparently it did, if an unknown voice on the telephone is any indication."

"They stopped a milk truck, you say? Somehow I knew it would *have* to be a milk truck. Spilling milk on the highway gets the public stirred up, because it seems especially hard on babies and invalids."

This suggestion started Ted thinking. "You mean you think the farmers deliberately put a milk truck through just to create a disturbance with the union?"

"Sure, why not? That's the idea, isn't it, to try to make the other side shoulder all the blame?"

Ted frowned. "I'm not saying you might not be right, but there're a couple of other things to remember, too. In the first place there isn't any strike so far, and in the second place maybe milk is the only thing the farmers have to ship at this season of the year—besides eggs, and I'm glad it isn't eggs. However, I don't want to blame either side until I find out what the score is."

Nelson suddenly asked, "What did you do with that film, Ted, return it to Mr. Prentice?"

"No, not yet. I called his office but he wasn't in. It's still here." He patted his pocket again.

"I don't like that very much, Ted. You never know what we might run into. Want me to lock it up in the glove compartment?"

"Well, maybe so as long as it's the only place we've got to lock it. Let's keep our eyes on it, though. I don't suppose a clever sneak thief would have much trouble with a lock like this."

He produced the film and locked it away, returning the key to Nelson's key case.

"Look, Ted, about these pictures. You can't just stick your camera in somebody's face and think you're going to get anything. We've got to sort of sneak up on the situation."

"You mean you're afraid somebody might try to stop us?"

"I don't know about that, but why give them the chance? Even if they don't object, at least they might stop doing what they're doing and start some innocent posing. That's why I'm glad I've got a candid camera and a distance lens."

"Well, how far away can we be and still get good pictures?"

"That depends on a lot of things—how clear the light is and what we're trying to catch. It's kind of an overcast day, but I've got some special fast film in my camera."

"They have to be especially clear if you want to use them for a newspaper, don't they?"

"Yes, because the newspapers use such coarse screens they dull the picture down. You can even see the big dots on a newspaper picture, if you look closely enough. Well, let's start as far away as we can, and then keep moving up closer until they spot us. Then we'll see what happens."

Nelson had slowed down as they approached the rioting. They were soon able to see this had been no crank call. Up ahead they saw a white milk truck overturned and partially blocking the highway. No policemen were on the scene so far, but there was a group of angry men milling around. They were spilling the milk out on the road, while the driver of the truck was apparently protesting loudly but ineffectively. The boys were still too far away to hear what was being said.

Nelson drew the car to a stop. "Let's get out here. There's a slight curve in the road. I think we can creep up over the crest of this hill on the side, and close in on them before they spot us."

With this Ted agreed. They got out of the car, and Nelson locked the doors after them. If the men farther down the road had seen them at all, they were paying no attention to them. Nelson's camera was carried in a sling at his side. The boys left the road, and climbed swiftly but quietly to the top of the hill. There they had a good view of the scene in front of them.

"How is this?" asked Ted.

"Borderline." Nelson grunted. "I might get it and I might not. Of course it will be easy enough to see the truck overturned, and the men around it. But you might not be sure what they're doing, and you won't be able to positively recognize anyone. Well, here goes nothing."

He took out his camera and focused it carefully. He snapped one picture, wound the film to the next exposure, and waiting a little longer took another.

"That's enough from here. Let's try to get a little closer."

They crept a little way down the hill, partially hidden by several trees and one or two of the cars lined up along the highway. Nelson got down on one knee and took another shot.

"Get it?" Ted inquired.

"I don't know. This distance lens of mine is tricky. It wasn't exactly made for my camera because I bought it separately. Anway, this'll have to do. We can't get any closer than this or they will see us."

"But maybe they won't try to stop us. We're privileged members of the press, remember?"

"Oh, I'm going to try some more, but these are the ones I'm counting on. Wait a minute," he called, for Ted, who had stooped beside him, had started to rise. "I want to put a different roll of film in the camera."

"Why? You didn't finish the old roll, did you?"

"Not by a long shot. But just the same I'd like to have a different film in the camera, and keep this other one safe if I can." He had a spare film in his pocket, and he quickly made the change. He was about to place the exposed film in his pocket when he hesitated. "How about *you* holding this one, Ted? They'll be less likely to suspect you, in case they try to stop us."

A willing conspirator, Ted accepted the film and placed it in his own pocket. Again he watched, almost admiringly, as Nelson set the indicator on his camera to read fifteen.

"That's so they won't realize I've just put in a new film," he explained.

Ted shook his head in wonder. "Boy, you're *real* sneaky, aren't you? I'm not sure I'd trust you any more."

"Why not? I'd rather trust somebody who uses his head than somebody who doesn't. Anything else going on?"

Several other cars were pulling up, but these appeared to contain merely spectators who were careful to stay back out of the way. And still no police officers had arrived although the wild-cat strikers were milling about, and it seemed possible the driver of the truck might be subject to physical violence. He was still arguing but was otherwise offering no resistance.

"A good thing for him," Nelson decided. "Why doesn't Mr. Dobson do something about this county police situation?"

"One crusade at a time," Ted cautioned. "Well, what are you waiting for?"

"Me? I thought I was waiting for you. Let's get out of the frying pan and into the fire."

He stood up and they started together down the hill.

CHAPTER 10

ROUGH HANDLING

THEIR APPROACH WAS SOON NOTICED. ONE OF the men looked up, then looked away again, and appeared to continue his conversation.

"He saw us, all right," Nelson whispered, "but he's waiting for us to get closer."

"Maybe he doesn't care," Ted whispered back hopefully, but somehow he found it difficult to believe this. That crowd of angry men looked unfriendly. If they were determined and angry enough to upset a milk truck, what would they do to anyone trying to report and photograph the scene?

When they had approached within fifty feet, the same man looked up again, broke away from the group, and came toward them with an air of determination.

"Is that a camera you're carrying there, sonny?"

Nelson made no answer, but continued on his way, until the man repeated:

"I asked you if that was a camera you're carrying."

"You said 'sonny,' " Nelson retorted, "so I thought you must be talking to someone else." He moved as though to go on, but the man barred his way.

"I was talking to you, all right, and you know it. That is a camera, isn't it?"

"Well, what if it is?"

"Did you take any pictures with it?"

"What if I did? I'm a photographer for a newspaper." He produced his press card with a flourish and showed it to the man. The latter read it and looked perplexed. He called to another man.

"Hey, he works for the newspaper." The second man came over to join this new discussion. He, too, studied the press card a moment, then turned to Ted.

"Do you work for the newspaper, too?"

"Yes." Ted also produced his press card and offered it for inspection. The man read it, then shook his head in disbelief.

"Boy, they must be taking them out of kindergarten this year." He turned back to Nelson. "Have you taken any pictures yet?"

"What if I have?" said Nelson.

"Check the indicator," the first man advised.

The second man, who gave the appearance of being the leader of the group, reached out his hand toward Nelson's case, but Nelson drew back.

"Listen, you know who I work for? Mr. Dobson, and he doesn't stand for any pushing around. You interfere with me and he'll keep you plastered on the front page till you'll wish you were never born."

The first man grabbed the leader's arm. "I've heard of this Dobson guy, and that's the way he works. We'd better be pretty careful, whatever we decide to do."

"I've got to see that indicator. Look, that much isn't going to hurt you, is it? I just want to see if you took any pictures, before I decide what to do. That looks like a pretty expensive camera, and you don't want it accidentally broken, do you? Then let me see it."

Once more he reached for the carrying case at Nelson's side. Protesting but not resisting, Nelson allowed him to take the camera from its case and find the indicator.

"He's taken fourteen pictures already. Did you take any of them here, or are these all from somewhere else?"

"I don't think that's any of your business," Nelson retorted.

"All right." He returned the camera to the case, then spoke to his friend. "See that they don't leave."

"Don't worry, *I'm* not leaving," Nelson called after him, as the leader left them to join the group of men.

It occurred to Ted that this might be a chance to make their escape, but he thought better of it. Besides the risk of injury to themselves and damage to Nelson's camera, there was the possibility of losing that precious film Ted was carrying in his pocket. The boys had to carry on their bluff in the hope of saving that film. Ted was glad that the microfilm, at least, was locked up in Nelson's car, a safe distance away.

The leader was huddled in a serious discussion with the rest of his men. The driver of the milk truck, meanwhile, had left the group and gone over to inspect the damage. Within a minute or so, the leader appeared to have reached a decision. He broke away from the group again, followed by two of the huskiest of his men. He approached Nelson directly.

"I'm sorry, kid, whatever your name is, but there's no way out of it. I've got to have that film. I don't want to hurt you, and I don't want to break your camera. I simply want that film. Now I'll tell you what I'll do. Just to show you I'm no crook, I'll *pay* you for that film." He took a dollar out of his pocket and handed it to Nelson, who threw it on the ground.

"What good does a dollar do me? What do I care about a film? It's the pictures *on* the film that count."

"Well, what's your price for the pictures?"

"What's my job worth?" said Nelson scornfully. "It's no pictures, no job."

"Sorry. I tried to buy the pictures, but you wouldn't give me a reasonable price. That means I'll have to take them by force, and you can explain to your boss that it wasn't your fault. Are you going to give me that film quietly, or do we have to work for it?"

"You're going to have to work for it," Nelson retorted.

The leader motioned toward the two large men behind him, who approached Nelson, and each grabbed an arm. Then Nelson struggled, squirmed, and kicked, meanwhile calling them every name he could think of. Even Ted, who knew it was all put on, had to marvel at his friend's performance. In fact, he began to wonder if perhaps it wasn't a little bit too real. Nelson had started out pretending, but now he seemed to be getting really mad. Film or no film, it's no fun to be held helpless while two big men help themselves to your possessions. There seemed to be a principle involved. Ted hoped fervently that Nelson wouldn't give the whole show away.

Finally Ted decided he ought to make at least some pretense of going to the aid of his friend. He started toward the struggling group, but the first man laid a strong grip on his arm. Ted tried to shake it off, but it was very firm. He continued to struggle, but not too much. He didn't know what he would do if the man suddenly decided to let go.

The leader managed to take Nelson's camera from its case, opened the back, and pulled out the roll of film, trailing it till it reached the ground. Having made sure that the film was entirely exposed, he closed up the camera, and returned it to its case.

"That's that. You can stop your kicking, kid. There's nothing you can do now that will bring that film back." He dropped the streamer on the ground and turned away. The other men released their grips, turned their backs on them and walked away.

"Well, we did it," Nelson muttered. "How was I?"

"Too bad somebody didn't take a movie of it. You'd have got the Academy Award sure."

"Pretty good, huh? That's because it wasn't *all* acting. I was really getting burned up. I'll bet my arms are all bruised."

"Hurt you much?" asked Ted.

"No. I've taken ten times as much as that in a football game. But that's different, because you can fight back. It's the feeling of being helpless that gets you down. I would have let go with everything I've got and put in at least a couple of good punches, if I hadn't known the film we really wanted was in your pocket all the time. Who's that coming?"

Another man they hadn't seen before came running up. They hadn't noticed where he came from, nor had they heard any new cars pulling up. Perhaps he had been inside one of the cars all along, or else he had walked up along the road. He delivered a quick message, and the leader snapped something to his men. After that there was a quick bustling about as they gathered together any of their possessions that were lying around, and hurried over to the cars, piled in, and drove off with a roar. Soon Ted and Nelson were standing there alone, except for the milk truck driver still ruefully examining his upset truck, and a half dozen spectators standing some distance away.

"He must have told them the police were on the way," Nelson speculated. "We should have gotten those license numbers, shouldn't we?"

Ted shrugged. "Probably wouldn't make any difference. I'll bet the licenses were all issued to people who can prove they were a hundred miles away from here at the time. You think you could identify any of these men?"

"Hm—no," Nelson decided. "They all had their hats pulled down over their faces, and there wasn't anything else about them I could recognize. But anyway I don't think I could identify any of them for certain, even if I did see them again—unless they left their thumb prints on my arms!"

"How many did you think there were?"

"Let's see—the first one, and the big shot he called over, and the two bruisers that held me, and about three others. That makes seven, doesn't it?"

"I'd call it eight, counting that man who came up at the end. Well, I guess we're still newspapermen working on a story. I'm going to talk to that truck driver. Are you going to take any pictures?"

"With what? Do you think I'm made of film?"

"You only took a few pictures on this roll in my pocket. Couldn't you put that back in the camera?"

"I wouldn't want to chance it, out here in the daylight. Those pictures are too valuable to risk—a lot better than just an overturned milk truck with the men all gone."

Ted started away. Nelson paused to pick up the dollar bill, and trotting to catch up with Ted, gave it to him. "There, that makes up for the dollar you gave Jerry. We'll come out even on that."

"What about your film?"

"I've got an expense account, haven't I?"

They walked over to the truck driver.

"Pretty bad," Ted commented.

"Yeah. It'll take a crane to right it, and at least a few hundred dollars' repairs. That's not counting the loss of the milk. Well, I don't see how they can blame me for it. All I did was what I was told to do."

"They told you to drive the truck through the lines?"

"Well, they didn't put it like that. There isn't any strike, you see. They told me to take this back road to avoid trouble if I could. But I couldn't. It seems those guys were there waiting for me, just as though they knew I was coming."

"Maybe they only suspected that *someone* would be coming," Ted suggested.

"But why a back road?" asked the driver.

"Why not? That would be the most logical place to watch, if they thought milk trucks were trying to squeeze through."

The man nodded glumly, but whether he agreed with Ted or not they couldn't tell.

"Are you a union member by any chance?" Ted inquired.

"Union? You crazy? If I were union, there wouldn't have been any trouble. I'm a free-wheeler. They said they couldn't get a union man to handle it, so they hired me. It's a job, isn't it? If they're having trouble that's no fault of mine."

"Did the men threaten you?"

"What do *you* think? They blocked the road and ordered me down out of my cab. If there's only one man, you can stand up to him, but when he's got six others with him, you have to listen."

"What would have happened if you'd resisted?"

"See what happened to the truck? The only difference is that I would have been in it."

"Would you care to give me your name, Mr.—?"

The driver looked up, startled. "Say, who are you?"

"I'm a reporter for the Forestdale *Town Crier*. My friend here is a photographer, but he's temporarily out of film."

"A reporter! You?" He squeezed his eyes to narrow slits. "I never guessed that. If I had, I wouldn't have opened my mouth so readily. No, I don't think I'd better give you my name. I don't know what the co-op. would say about it. Anyway, I'd just as soon keep my own name out of the papers. There's no percentage in that."

"Wouldn't you like to get your side of the story into print?"

"Sure, I would. But can't you report what I said without using my name?"

Ted looked dubious. "I can try, but I doubt whether Mr. Dobson will use it. He doesn't go much for anonymous statements, especially when even *he* doesn't know the name of the person who made them. There's no way to test how reliable they are."

The driver motioned toward the overturned truck. "That's a good test of my reliability, isn't it?"

Although Ted asked him again, he still refused to give his name, and believing the man wasn't going to change his mind, Ted finally gave up. Nor did he think having a camera with film would help much, for the man would undoubtedly have refused to be photographed. Maybe they could get the driver's name later from the co-operative, though that probably wouldn't be in time for their next issue. They hoped to put the paper to bed soon after noon.

"I can come back for a picture of that truck later," Nelson remarked to Ted as they walked away, "if Mr. Dobson wants it. It'll depend on how my other pictures turn out. I think one of my other shots will be better, showing the truck with the men around it. I don't suppose the paper can use more than one or two pictures anyway."

Ted decided to stop to talk to the other spectators, some of whom were just getting ready to leave. But one and all reacted in the same way. When they learned he was a newspaper reporter, they refused to talk for publication.

"Why should I get mixed up in this?" one man remarked. "I'm a union man myself—not the trucking union, of course. Anyway, I didn't really see anything. It was all over by the time I got here."

"Could you identify any of the men?"

"Of course not. This is as close as I got. How could I recognize anyone from here?"

Everyone else also denied having been there at the time the truck was overturned, although Ted felt certain some of them must have been. Of course no one admitted recognizing any of the men.

"Well, I tried," Ted remarked, as they trudged back toward their car.

"Now I know the kind of trouble reporters have getting a story. These wild-catters think they're right, but they're afraid to stand up and be counted. These witnesses are afraid to admit what they saw. The truck driver is afraid of sticking his neck out. Nobody's willing to make a stand on principle, any more. I think that's the trouble with the whole world."

"Let's say it's *one* of the troubles of the whole world," said Ted with a ghost of a smile. They got into the car and headed back toward Forestdale.

CHAPTER 11

TED'S NOTORIETY

OPENING THE GLOVE COMPARTMENT WITH Nelson's key, Ted took out the roll of microfilm and put it in his coat pocket.

"Where to now, Ted?" Nelson questioned.

"Drop me off at Mr. Waring's. He should be in by now. If not, I guess I'll leave it with his secretary after all. She ought to be reliable enough, and she'll surely realize how important it is."

"Want me to wait for you?"

"No, thanks, I might get to talking with Mr. Waring, and I don't know how long it might take. I can walk to the office from there, easily enough."

"What time are you going to get off work?"

"Who knows on a Saturday? We're never scheduled for work on a Saturday afternoon, but somehow it usually manages to turn out that way. And I want to clear up everything I can, as long as this is my last day on the newspaper."

"It was kind of fun, wasn't it, Ted? It was a good thing for you Carl Allison was out of town."

"No, I guess Mr. Dobson might not have needed me if he had been here, and then I might have spent my whole vacation loafing. Wouldn't that have been terrible?"

Nelson grinned, knowing this crack was meant for him. He didn't object to work, but liked to do some grumbling first so that people would appreciate his efforts all the more.

"What are you going to do this afternoon?" Ted asked him.

"I want to get this film in the developing bath as soon as I can, so I can see what I have. I'll call you at the office when I get finished, and you can tell Mr. Dobson. Then maybe I can pick you up."

"Pick me up? And then what?"

"I don't know. Whatever you say. Got any ideas?"

"Yes," said Ted slowly. "I'd sort of like to go out to see the scavenger again."

"What for? You've got the microfilm. What else can he do for us?"

"I don't know—nothing probably. It's just that I've suddenly become suspicious of everybody. I'd just like to find out if he's everything he seems to be."

"You think he'll tell you?"

"No, but we can snoop around a little and see what we can find out."

Nelson grinned. "I know. You want to see if you can find that million dollars he buried."

They were on Mr. Waring's street by this time. Ted turned into the entrance of Mr. Waring's building and mounted the stairs.

"Is Mr. Waring in?" he inquired of the secretary.

"Yes, Ted, he is. I'll buzz him."

Over the intercommunication system she explained to Mr. Waring that Ted was there. In the inner office, Mr. Waring came forward to shake Ted's hand. Then Ted produced the film from his pocket. There was no mistaking the relieved look on the attorney's face.

"You got it, Ted? That's a real break for us. If we'd only had it yesterday morning, we could have kept Judge Harder from cracking the whip over our heads. I'll have to telephone Mr. Prentice the good news, and have him call off his hunt. He's in a mad race trying to get all those documents together again and photographed before Tuesday morning. He'll be glad to know now that he doesn't have to."

"Are you sure this will help Mr. Prentice so much, Mr. Waring?" asked Ted slowly.

"What do you mean, Ted?"

Ted did not want to admit that he had examined the film, since it might appear to the attorney that he had been snooping. He said simply: "Well, what if there was something on the film that would be unfavorable to Mr. Prentice's case?"

"Oh, there couldn't be, Ted. I'm sure that if there were Mr. Prentice would have told me about it in advance. If—"

He was interrupted by the buzz of the intercommunication system. "Long-distance call, Mr. Waring."

"Oh, yes, put it through. Excuse me, Ted."

"Certainly. I'll be going now, Mr. Waring."

"All right, then, thank you, Ted. I'm very much obliged to you."

Back at the office, Ted wrote up the story of the overturned milk truck. As he had expected, Mr. Dobson, who was more particular about such things than most editors, refused to quote the anonymous truck driver, nor would he allow the rioters to be identified as union men. This left Ted with a watered-down version that was little better than no story at all.

It would just about make a caption for a picture, he thought privately. Nelson might have a picture, but when he asked Mr. Dobson about it, the editor said:

"No, Ted, we might as well wait on that. We're running short of space and time, and I'm sure there'll be more developments next week. The picture will still be timely then, and perhaps we can get a few facts to back it up so it won't be so vague."

With their holiday deadline creeping up on them, they all worked right through the lunch hour. Shortly after that Nelson phoned.

"Ted, are you ready to leave yet?"

"In about half an hour, I guess." He held his hand over the mouthpiece as Mr. Dobson spoke to him, then relayed the message to Nelson. "Mr. Dobson says to bring in your time and expense sheet, so that he can give you a check."

"Does he know about the pictures, Ted? I've put them through the developer, and I think they're going to turn out fine."

"He said he'd hold any pictures up till next week."

"O.K., Ted. I'll pick you up in half an hour."

Ted was ready by the time Nelson arrived. Ted already had his check, and there was a short delay while another one was prepared for Nelson. He turned in his press card with considerable reluctance.

"There might be a fire on the road to Echo," he reminded the editor.

"Well, we'll hope there isn't," said Mr. Dobson with a smile. "I appreciate the way you boys filled in during vacation. Happy New Year, and don't study too hard at college."

"I won't," Nelson promised with full sincerity.

"Happy New Year, Mr. Dobson," Ted called. "Happy New Year, Miss Monroe."

"Thank you. Take care of yourself, Ted."

They stopped along the road for lunch, and then continued to Echo. Ted was feeling more relaxed than he had in some days, now that his newspaper chores were ended, and he had nothing to do but enjoy himself until Tuesday morning. That microfilm had been a weight on his mind, too, but now he had delivered it to Mr. Waring, and it was up to the lawyer to decide what to do next. He didn't feel they were on an errand of great urgency now, but one inspired mostly by curiosity.

"You know what I'm going to do tonight?" Ted announced lazily. "I'm going to loaf—that's all, just loaf. Maybe read a little, or watch television, and stay up as late as I please. Then sleep late tomorrow morning, mosey around in the afternoon, and go to the party tomorrow night. Sleep till noon Monday, and watch the football games on TV until it's time to pack my suitcase."

"Nice going," said Nelson with some sarcasm. "You can do it because you don't have a houseful of kids. If they bring their friends over the way they usually do, I'll have about fifteen of them in my hair."

"That's what you get for being the oldest child in the family."

"A fat lot I had to say about it. How are you going to handle this scavenger, Ted?"

"I don't know yet. Maybe I won't even talk to him at all, but just try to get a glimpse of his set-up."

Nelson turned off the main road and took the rough dirt road leading to the dump, which saved them some walking time. They got out and looked around, but saw nothing particularly novel. It was just a dump, but there was no activity going on just then. Either the men didn't work on Saturday afternoons, or else they had been given extra time off for the holidays. Ted was a little disappointed.

"I thought I might meet somebody I could talk to, and ask about the scavenger. Well, there's no help for it. Let's wander over toward his shack."

"I don't see his truck. Maybe he's gone again. I suppose even a scavenger takes off for the holidays."

"That might be just as well. Then I won't have to make up an excuse in case he sees us."

"You don't need any excuse, Ted. You're a newspaper reporter, remember? Just tell him you're working on a feature story about this kind of life."

"Who'd read it?"

"That's not the right attitude, Ted. A real newspaperman never knows where a story's going to pop up. I even thought of asking to take his picture but I decided against it. It gets too complicated. If I wanted to send the picture to a magazine, I'd have to get a signed release from him, and all that jazz. You don't have that trouble on a newspaper, do you?"

"No, not if you can show there's a legitimate public interest in your pictures. Of course that doesn't give you the right to creep up on people's houses and take pictures through the windows. I guess if a person poses willingly for a newspaper picture, that means he's given his consent to having it published. I think you're right about his being gone, though. Say, isn't that door a little bit ajar?"

"Yes, it is. What do you think it means, Ted?"

"If it means what I think it means, he's flown the coop—permanently. I don't think we can see anything through that window. Want to open the door?"

"You told me last time that was burglary," Nelson complained.

"No, not if the door's left open and we think it's empty. I don't see any harm in opening the door all the way to check. Push it open, but don't go in, and don't take anything—not even a deep breath."

Nelson did so, and they saw at once that the shack had been abandoned. Everything that could be considered of any value had been removed, and all that was left was the makeshift furniture, some odds and ends on the shelves, and the usual rubbish that people leave behind them. There was no reason now why they shouldn't go in, and the boys did so. They rummaged through the shack but without finding anything to give them a clue as to the scavenger's identity or the reason for his sudden departure.

"Maybe he just got tired of working," Nelson remarked. "Other men quit their jobs. Why shouldn't he?"

"On the other hand, why should he—just when people are looking for him?"

"Who's looking for him?"

"We are. And there might be other people, too, who would be interested in knowing just how he found that microfilm."

"You mean Mr. Prentice might try to lie about it?"

"Let's not say that yet. We'll give him a chance and see."

"Maybe that's exactly why the scavenger did leave right now," Nelson observed. "Maybe he felt he was getting mixed up in something, and he didn't want to. I suppose you can get his name from somewhere, can't you?"

"I imagine so. The dump owners must have it. You probably have to pay for a concession like this one."

"You *pay* for it?" said Nelson incredulously.

"Sure, the way a hatcheck girl sometimes has to pay for her job in a night club."

"Boy, everybody's got some sort of racket, haven't they?"

There seemed nothing further for them to do there, and they left the shack just as they found it. Still, it was pleasant just to be outside, in the clear, brisk, wintry weather, and they wandered around for a while longer before getting back into the car.

Back at home, Ted learned there had been a telephone call for him. It was from Mr. Waring.

"He was very polite, Ted," Mrs. Wilford related. "He said he had been too rushed to thank you properly this morning. He also said that he'd had a chance to go over the film very carefully, and he was sure there was nothing on it that would hurt Mr. Prentice."

Ted felt miserable. He felt sure now that Mr. Prentice and Mr. Waring were going to lie about that microfilm. All right, then, let them, he thought savagely, and if they got caught it was their funeral. At least Mr. Dobson had convinced him that it wasn't any of *his* affair, and he shrugged the whole thing off—or tried to.

While waiting for his mother to prepare supper, Ted picked up the evening daily from the city, and turned to the front page. There he was startled to see his own name, linked to a far from favorable story—

CHAPTER 12

THE MAN WITH THE RAISED SHOULDER

THE ARTICLE IN THE NEWSPAPER WAS UNDER the by-line of Jim Horner. He was one of their best-known reporters. He was often accused of having an anti-union bias, but he had his staunch supporters as well. Ted's impression was that Horner tried to be accurate in his reporting so that whatever he said was generally true. His bias was shown by the fact that he looked for stories that reflected upon the unions rather than management. But maybe that was just his specialty, Ted had thought, for one reporter can't do everything.

Horner's story told of the court hearing on the previous day—which was old news by now, but it was pegged on a new angle. It said there had been a postponement of the court hearing due to the disappearance of the microfilm. This film, the story said, was in the possession of Ted Wilford, reporter for the Forestdale *Town Crier.* A few other facts about Ted followed, all of them true as far as they went, but designed to emphasize his youth and inexperience. There was the implication that Ted had allowed himself to be used as the tool of the union interests. His close association with Mr. Prentice was mentioned. Ted felt his cheeks growing crimson with indignation as he read.

He called his mother and showed the story to her. She did not see anything so bad about the references to him. True, he was young and without a great deal of experience, but to her it was a compliment that he had had the chance to report the story in spite of these handicaps.

"Don't you see, Mom, he doesn't mention the time element. A person reading this story can get the impression that the film was in my possession on Friday morning, and that I deliberately held it in spite of the court order. I could get into serious trouble that way."

Then Mrs. Wilford understood, too, and was almost as indignant as Ted was. "But I don't see how you can be in any real trouble, Ted. As long as you haven't done anything wrong, and you tell the truth about it, everything will be all right."

Ted almost smiled. "Thanks, Mom. I hope you're right. But even if you aren't, I wouldn't want any other kind of mother."

There was an indignant call from Nelson as soon as the story had also caught his eye.

"Some crust, Ted. Isn't there anything you can do about it, or do you just have to sit and take an attack like that?"

"I don't know what there is to do. It'll probably all come out right in court Tuesday morning. Mr. Waring can tell when I got the film, and when I gave it to him—" He stopped, remembering suddenly that on the basis of Mr. Waring's call it seemed likely that the lawyer was going to lie in court. And if he wanted to lie about what was on the film, might he not also lie about the time Ted gave it to him?

"Well, I don't like it one little bit, Ted. The funny thing about it is that the whole story is true, except for that one detail about when you got the film. But it still gives a nasty picture, doesn't it? I wonder how he found out you had the film. I didn't tell anybody. Did you?"

"Oh, no, I hardly told anyone at all. Let's see who knows about it. Just you and me, and the scavenger, and Mr. and Mrs. Speck, and Mr. Dobson and Miss Monroe, and Mr. Waring and his secretary, and anybody else that any of these people happened to mention it to. I wouldn't call that a very well-kept secret."

"The scavenger might have told him. That Jim Horner has been getting news leaked to him from some sources, and the scavenger might be one of them. Or Mr. and Mrs. Speck might have told him, if he had asked them. They wouldn't have seen any reason not to tell."

"What about the photographer?" asked Ted suddenly. "I don't think Jim Horner misses any bets. He might have learned we borrowed a projector, and put two and two together from that."

"I'll bet that's it, Ted. Want me to check with him?"

"No, what's the use? The harm's all done now."

"It just goes to show, doesn't it, how a story can be true or almost true, and still be all wrong at the same time. It all depends on the interpretation you want to put on it. Reading that story, I'd think you were on the union payroll, and yet it doesn't say that."

"No," said Ted dejectedly, "but it might just as well."

They continued to exchange bitter comments, but it led nowhere, and eventually they hung up. Ted received another call that evening. This one was from Ken Kutler.

"Tough luck, Ted. Jim Horner sure took you for a ride tonight."

"You can play that record again. What can you do when somebody prints something about you that isn't quite true?"

"You mean that the story isn't true, Ted?"

"The most important detail isn't. I *didn't* have that film on Friday morning. Of course he didn't really say that I did. It just sounds like it."

"Bad, Ted, bad. I don't think there's anything you can hold him to on that, even if you had any witnesses, which I don't suppose you do."

"Just Nelson, and a man who seems to have disappeared."

"Well, Ted, that's rough. But that's not really the worst part of his story. It's the interpretation it puts on your actions. As far as interpretations go, I guess a reporter is allowed pretty much latitude, unless you can pin him down on a false fact. It isn't responsible journalism, but I imagine Jim Horner really believes what he says."

"And so will most of his readers," Ted added.

"I hope it clears up for you, Ted. A reputation like that can follow you wherever you go in the journalism field. Well, I didn't call to pump you for information, just to offer you a little sympathy. And I've also got something to tell you. Don't worry, I'm not giving away any stories. You won't be able to use this, because the principal person concerned will deny it. But didn't you think Mr. Abbott's attitude was rather strange, at that conference in your office yesterday morning?"

"Yes, I did."

"That wasn't like Mr. Abbott. Oh, he's entitled to his opinions, all right. But that attack at the end on Mr. Prentice's character was way out of line. I know what's back of it, though. Mr. Abbott has been receiving anonymous telephone calls and letters threatening his family."

"He has! But surely he doesn't think Mr. Prentice is responsible for them."

"No, not really. But he thinks the union is irresponsible and can't control its own men. So he's sure someone in the union is back of it, whether Mr. Prentice happens to know of it or not. Of course, you can say you don't have to pay attention to cowardly threats of that kind, but you can't forget them that easily. I think he's both worried about his family and disgusted with the union. If this strike comes, he may just decide to pull out of his business and retire. That wouldn't help the unions much, either. The next man might be even tougher to deal with."

After that call Ted could not settle down to the quiet evening he had planned. Neither a book nor television could hold his attention for long. He tuned in to the late news, and learned that the union had called an unusual Sunday morning meeting, where it was expected a strike vote would be taken. The truckers might be out before the New Year's bells rang.

He spent another restless night. At noon on Sunday he turned on another news report to get the latest developments on the strike situation. It seemed there had been a majority feeling in favor of a strike, but that Mr. Prentice personally intervened, and asked that a strike vote be delayed. This was done, but there was some doubt he would be able to hold all the members in line, and that further incidents like the overturned milk truck might develop. It was thought that Mr. Prentice might seek to postpone a strike until the court hearing was over, on the ground that two things coming at once would cast the union in too unfavorable a light in the newspapers. With this Ted could well agree, if the letters on the microfilm were ever made public.

Still restless, Ted walked over to Nelson's home that afternoon. Nelson was working in his darkroom in the basement. Ted had to wait until he opened the door of his room, for he had a lock on the inside to avoid interruptions at critical moments.

"Those riot pictures turned out fine," he reported. "They're better than you would expect with a candid camera and a distance lens that doesn't quite fit. Take a look at 'em, Ted."

Ted did so, and felt in spite of the camera and their position on the hill, they had come out very well.

"These ought to do for the newspaper—at least this one." Ted stopped, and examined one of the pictures more closely.

"What's the matter with it?" his friend inquired.

"Nothing that I know of. But look—this man standing here. Doesn't he look a little bit peculiar?"

"Yes, I noticed that. He's standing with one shoulder a little higher than the other. I don't think he's crippled, or anything like that. Some people just have that peculiarity."

"I know, I've seen some of them. Just the same, doesn't he look a little bit familiar to you?"

"Hm? No, I can't exactly say that he does."

"You haven't seen anybody else who stands like that in the last couple of days?"

"No, not that I remember."

"Not the scavenger, maybe?" Ted shot out at him.

"The scavenger! Hm, I remember now, he did stand a little bit that way. But what would the scavenger be doing at a union riot?"

"Or what would a union rioter be doing as a scavenger?" asked Ted with a smile. "What do you think?" he asked, as Nelson studied the photo once more.

"I said the picture was good, but I didn't say it was *that* good. This was a distant shot, and it shows a whole group of men and an overturned truck. How can you identify one man as the scavenger?"

"Oh, I didn't say for *sure*. I just said it looked like him."

"You mean you think the scavenger is a straw man—somebody who isn't what he pretends to be?"

"I don't know—I wish I did. But we know that the scavenger wasn't at his shack on Saturday, the day the riot took place, so that proves he was somewhere else!"

"Now that's a startling deduction if I ever heard one. Do you know that the world is a pretty big place—twenty-five thousand miles around and it weighs umpty trillion tons?"

"All right, all right. All I meant was that it was *possible* for him to have been at the riot scene, as far as we know."

"And a few million other places, too." He squinted down at the picture once more. "I say, though, Ted, this is kind of eerie, but it looks to me now that maybe this *is* the scavenger. Of course he's wearing different clothes, and you can't see much of his face with that hat on. But his general build and carriage are about the same. Oh, what's the use? This picture isn't clear enough to tell for sure, and maybe we're just imagining things. How many people do you know who stand with one shoulder higher than the other?"

"None that I've seen lately—except the scavenger."

"What are we going to do about that guy, Ted? It seems as though we just can't get rid of him. He's always popping up to bother us. You want to do anything more about trying to find him? You thought we could check with the dump owners."

"Sure, we could, if we had time. But where are we going to find them over a holiday weekend? There's something we could do, though, maybe. We could drive out to Echo tomorrow afternoon and show this picture to Jerry Speck. He knew the scavenger better than we did, and might be able to identify him."

"Take it easy, Ted. You've got to be cautious when you deal with kids. That Jerry's got a good imagination, and I don't know how well you could rely on what he says. Anyway, I'm not sure even Jerry could tell from this picture."

"Well, maybe. It was just an idea."

"We'll see, Ted. It'll depend on how things are going and how tired we are. Believe me, I hate that newspaper story just as much as you do, but I'm not sure that finding the scavenger is going to do you any good. We said Friday, when he turned down the reward, that he might have some secrets of his own that he didn't want aired, and that still seems the most likely explanation. You want him to step forward and swear to the time when he gave you that film, but I'm not sure he'd be willing to do it, even if we did find him."

And Ted had to admit that this was probably right. Whether the scavenger had disappeared because of some secrets of his own, or simply because he felt like it, he probably wouldn't come to Ted's defense. Chances were that he would deny he had ever seen them! Certainly he wouldn't want to be accused of stealing the microfilm from Mr. Prentice's car, particularly if it proved to be quite valuable, as it must now appear to him.

"How's the strike situation going?" asked Nelson, beginning to clean up some of his mess.

"Postponed—for as long as Mr. Prentice can keep the men in line."

"Every delay helps. You all ready for our own scavenger hunt tonight?"

"As ready as I'm going to be. What are the ground rules?"

"We're going to hunt in pairs, of course. We're not allowed to go outside the town limits of Forestdale, and everybody has to be back by midnight. The mothers have prepared the lists, and they say they know for a fact that everything on the lists is available somewhere in Forestdale."

"Then our only job is to find them," said Ted with a laugh. "You finished here?"

"Just about. I don't mean to give you the bum's rush, Ted, but I've got to drive some of the kids over to a party in North Ridge. Come along for the ride, if you want to."

"No, thanks, I'll be taking off. See you tonight. I guess we'll have fun on the scavenger hunt, all right, but I'd rather find the real scavenger."

CHAPTER 13

THE SCAVENGER HUNT

TED CALLED AT MARGARET'S HOME A LITTLE before eight
o'clock, and her father gave him his car keys. Helen Howland's home
was only a short distance away and they could easily have walked,
but the car would be useful for the scavenger hunt later. Then Margaret came downstairs, and they set off for the party.

A dozen old friends met at Helen's home. They had all been in
Forestdale High School, but some of them had not met since Septem-
ber so they had plenty to talk over. Helen soon clapped her hands for
attention.

"Let's get started on the hunt, or we won't be back before midnight. There'll be plenty of time for talk after that. Each couple's list
is different, so to make it fair we'll draw them out of a hat. And do
your best to win, because there's a *very nice* prize."

The girls each drew a list, and turned them over to their respec-
tive partners for consultation. A chorus of objections soon began to
arise.

"A forty-nine-star flag!" Cliff Corby exclaimed. "Where can we
find one of those? Everybody I know waited for the fifty-star flag to
come out."

"What's this 1909 penny? That's not an Indian head, is it? Those
things are scarcer than hen's teeth."

"How about a 1927 license plate? I thought people all drove
horses in those days."

"And where are we going to find a ten-year-old newspaper? Everybody I know cleans their shelves oftener than that. You've got
influence down at the *Town Crier*, Ted. Can you let us in there?"

"No, the papers in the files can't be taken out."

Ted and Margaret thought it best not to disclose their items to the
others, but some of the articles astonished them. Where were they

going to find an octopus in Forestdale? Surely that must have been intended as a joke, wasn't it?

"I wonder if they want a live octopus or a dead one," Ted whispered, "or would just a picture of one do?"

"No, I think they mean a real octopus. Do you know anybody who keeps a sea aquarium?"

"No, I don't, and if they did I don't think an octopus would be an easy thing to raise. Besides, how would we get it back here?"

"Well, we'll have to think about it. We must have picked the hardest list." But judging by some of the other comments they heard as they were leaving, the others were saying exactly the same thing.

They decided to get the easiest things first, just in case they might find time running out on them. A baby picture of the mayor offered no particular obstacles, other than the nerve to go and ask for it, and they drove over to his house. However, they found a carload of guests just arriving.

"Should we try it anyway?" asked Ted. "We could come back later, if you wanted to."

"Oh, I think it will be all right for us to ask for it now. But let's wait a couple of minutes until the guests get settled. How have you been doing on the newspaper, Ted? I thought I recognized several stories of yours in Friday's *Town Crier,* even though they weren't signed." She and Ted had worked together on the high-school paper, so they were familiar with each other's style. "That kitten in the mailbox was your story, wasn't it?"

"Yes. And did you like the one about the woman collecting Crackerjack prizes?"

"Oh, yes, that was cute. I'll bet you wrote up that false burglar alarm in the tea shop, too."

"That's right, I did. I forgot about that."

"What have you been doing the last few days, Ted—anything exciting?"

"Oh, there've been a couple of things. Maybe you've heard that Mr. Prentice was in an accident Thursday afternoon. A microfilm with some union records on it was missing from the car. Nelson and I drove out the next day, and we got it back. It seems that a dump scavenger had picked it up out of curiosity."

He did not go on to explain his own suspicions concerning the scavenger and his subsequent disappearance. Nor did he tell her about the letters he and Nelson had seen on the microfilm. It was too early to mention anything like that.

"Is that the film Jim Horner was talking about in the paper? I didn't like his story very much. Even if it was true, he didn't have any right to write it the way he did."

"His insinuations were wrong," said Ted philosophically, "but it'll all come out in the wash. Want to go in now?"

The mayor was not only glad to receive them, but introduced them to some of his guests. Then he got out an old album, and pointed out what he thought were the best pictures.

"I want to be sure you get an attractive one," he explained with a laugh.

They made their selection, and after thanking him and promising to return the picture, soon left.

Several more items on their list proved to be fairly easy because they happened to know where they could be found. But to find a book autographed by Ernest Hemingway proved frustrating. They stopped at the home of the librarian, and she stated that she didn't know of any such book in Forestdale. Of course it might be in almost any private home, but if they went around asking at random it was likely to take the whole evening, and might not produce the book in the end. They decided not to pursue the book for the time being, but simply to ask about it wherever they happened to go.

Margaret read the next item on the list. "A watch chain. That shouldn't be too hard. All the men used to wear them. Do you know where we can get one, Ted?"

"I don't even know anybody who wears a vest, let alone a watch chain," said Ted, laughing. "Everybody I know depends on a wristwatch, except for a railroad engineer, and he carries a clock. We ought to be able to find one, though. I suppose a lot of people have them stuck away in old jewelry boxes. That'll be easier than finding a scarecrow anywhere in town. I don't know anybody who's got one of *them* stuck away in a closet. Maybe they expect us to make one of our own."

"No, I don't think so. Everything on the lists is supposed to be available. Anyway, where would you find any straw? Oh, Ted—that watch chain. I think I know someone who wears one—Mr. Halliday. I'm pretty sure I saw him wearing it at church a few weeks ago."

"That so? I'd like to stop over and see him, but—"

"But what, Ted?"

"Well, he's sort of an old family friend, and I always try to see him during my vacations. I haven't made it so far because I know he's busy, and I've been busy, too. So if we did drop over I wouldn't want him to think I was just asking for a favor. I'd like to stay and talk a little while, and that might delay us on the scavenger hunt."

"I wouldn't mind, Ted. It would be nice to win the hunt, but we're only doing it for fun."

"Thanks, Margaret. This takes a load off my mind, because tomorrow is my last day in town, and I'd hate to miss him then. I don't believe you know him very well, but he's a wonderful man."

"I'm sure he is, Ted. I've never heard anything except the best about him."

They found, however, that Mr. Halliday also had guests. After a brief consultation they decided to go in just the same. It would be easy enough to ask about the watch chain, and if there was no chance to talk just then, Ted thought perhaps he could make an engagement for the following day.

Mr. Halliday, who was a widower and lived alone, answered the door himself.

"Well, Ted—and Margaret. This is a real pleasure. Won't you come in?"

Just as the mayor had done, he introduced them to his guests. There was a general exchange of good wishes.

"We're on a scavenger hunt, Mr. Halliday," said Ted when he had a chance to speak quietly with him, "and I thought this might be a good chance to see you."

"I'm glad you stopped by tonight, Ted. Let's take a look at that list. What was it that you thought I might have?"

"A watch chain," Margaret informed him. "Didn't I see you wearing one a few weeks ago?"

"Quite likely you did, Margaret. I'm afraid you're too late, though. I've just recently lost it—I can't imagine where. What else do you need on your list? An octopus? I'm sorry, but I've never kept one. An Ernest Hemingway autograph? I can't help you with that, either. Oh, say, what's this? A scarecrow? Why, I know where you can get that—or at least I think I do. You know that old barn that I've got at the edge of town? Of course I don't use it for a barn any more, but it's used occasionally for barn dances and things like that. The last time I was out there was on Halloween, for a Boy Scout party, and I recall that they had a scarecrow dressed up for decoration. It's still out there, as far as I know."

Ted snapped his fingers. "Why didn't I think of that? That's the only barn inside the limits of Forestdale, so if we are going to get a scarecrow anywhere, that's the place. Is the barn locked?"

"Yes, but I can give you the key. Or better yet, why don't I ride along with you? It's a pretty big place, and I might be able to find it more easily than you can."

"Your guests—" Ted reminded him.

"Oh, I'm sure they'll excuse me for a little while. They know my predilection for games."

Mr. Halliday made his excuses to his guests, put on his coat and hat, and left the house with them. It was not a very long ride, and soon the barn itself loomed up big and empty and ominous. Ted was just as glad to have Mr. Halliday along to help in the search. The barn was wired for electricity, and after unlocking the door, Mr. Halliday switched on the lights.

"This is a real fine place for a Halloween party," Ted remarked.

"Yes, I think so. I'm sure they had a good time. It's a shame that the youngsters of today have to miss out on some of the fun we used to have. I don't know any better place for children to play than in a big, old barn. Well, if my recollection is correct, we'll find the scarecrow in this old feed room over here."

Since Margaret was dressed for a party, she might have hesitated to walk through an old, dusty barn with hanging cobwebs and wisps of straw everywhere about. But she was as intrigued with the eerie setting as Ted, and eagerly followed the others into the feed room. The scarecrow was there, and Mr. Halliday hauled him into the main room so they could get a better look at him.

He was a most attractive scarecrow, after the dust was shaken off and some of his inwards stuffed back inside his clothes. The suit he was wearing was unpatched and even serviceable.

"How cute!" Margaret exclaimed. "He'll be the hit of our party."

"He's the best-dressed scarecrow I've ever seen," Ted decided. "I've seen worse clothes on hoboes. Do you want us to bring him back tomorrow?"

"Oh, no, no, I'm sure he's fulfilled all his duties and can reasonably be retired to rest. Do anything you please with him."

When they had returned to Mr. Halliday's house, Ted thanked him once more. "We surely appreciate your taking this trouble for us, Mr. Halliday."

"Oh, no trouble at all, Ted. I'm glad you called on me. Good night, Margaret. Good luck, Ted. Write to me once in a while, won't you?"

"I will, Mr. Halliday," Ted pledged. "Happy New Year!"

"I'm glad we stopped," Margaret remarked as they drove on. "I don't mean just for the scarecrow. I think he really was happy to see us. Ted—the octopus!"

"What about it, Margaret?"

"I think I know where we may be able to get one. Our biology teacher at high school had a hobby of embedding biological specimens in plastic. I never saw an octopus, but he had a lot of other things, and it wouldn't be surprising if he had that, too."

"Could be. Sounds like as good a chance as we're likely to have. Where else would we get an octopus? And we know there must be one."

They found their old biology teacher was still up, even though he had no visitors.

"Yes, I do have an octopus," he told them. "One of my best specimens. I didn't make a practice of showing it in school, since the girls were likely to be squeamish."

Their former teacher brought out his plastic-enclosed octopus and turned it over to them. Ted examined it with interest, and Margaret asked to hold the block, too. In spite of all the horror stories they had heard about this creature, it seemed unusually small and pathetic.

"This is wonderful," said Ted enthusiastically. "We'll bring it back tomorrow. Thank you for letting us borrow it. By the way, I don't suppose you have a watch chain, or an Ernest Hemingway autograph?"

"No, I'm afraid not. Happy New Year. I enjoyed seeing you again."

"Happy New Year," they called to him as they left the house.

"That's eight things. What do you want to do about the other two, Margaret?"

"Oh, why don't we let them go, Ted? Eight is pretty good—maybe good enough to win. Anyway, it's after eleven o'clock already. Let's get back and see how everybody else is doing."

They left the scarecrow out on the front porch, since Mrs. Howland wasn't likely to appreciate straw scattered through the house. They were not the first to return to the party, but they discovered no couple had been successful in finding all ten items on their lists.

Everyone was back just before twelve o'clock. Television was switched on, and they watched in silence as the clock on the screen moved toward twelve. At the stroke of midnight there was a shout and exchange of greetings, followed by the singing of *Auld Lang Syne* in unison with the television audience.

Then the judging began. Items were examined and exclaimed over, and finally approved. Nelson and his partner had returned with only six things, and the next couple had seven. Some of the others had given up in frustration. Ted's and Margaret's eight items were approved, but Cliff and his partner claimed to have nine. One by one they produced their loot, finally displaying a forty-nine-star flag with considerable pride.

"And you don't know the trouble we had getting it," Cliff declared.

"That's not a forty-nine-star flag," Nelson corrected.

"What do you mean it isn't? Count 'em. Forty-nine stars."

"Sure, but it's not the official American flag. Look how the stars are blocked. On the official flag the rows were staggered."

"That's right," Ted agreed. "I guess some of the flag manufacturers did jump the gun, before they found out the official design."

"What do you mean?" Cliff yelped. "It's an American flag, and it's got forty-nine stars on it. What more do you want?"

In the end, the judges decided to give Cliff half credit for his flag. Since he had produced eight and a half items, he and his partner were declared the winners, though Nelson still objected:

"How can you get half credit for a flag? Either it is a flag, or it isn't."

The prize was a five-gallon freezer of ice cream, and the winners were given the privilege of dishing it out.

After eating, they played games, listened to records, and danced. Finally it was time to go, and as Ted drove Margaret home, they agreed the scavenger hunt had been a lot of fun, especially finding the straw man.

CHAPTER 14

EVERY MAN A KING

IN SPITE OF GETTING TO BED LATE, TED WAS awakened very early by his mother.

"There's a man here to see you, Ted."

Ted looked sleepily at the clock. It was only a little after seven. He slipped on his robe and slippers and went downstairs.

"Are you Ted Wilford?" the man questioned him.

"Yes."

"I am a process server. Here is a subpoena to appear in Judge Harder's courtroom tomorrow morning at nine o'clock."

He turned and left without another word. Apparently he didn't expect Ted to thank him.

"I suppose they want to know just when I found the microfilm," Ted told his mother. He examined the paper carefully, and found that his appearance was requested by Mr. Davis, the prosecuting attorney. This meant that Ted was to testify against. Mr. Prentice's side. Ted had valued his friendship with the union leader, until he discovered those letters. Since then he had felt it was just as well not to be too closely allied with Mr. Prentice.

The telephone rang, and when Ted answered he heard Nelson's indignant voice.

"I suppose you got a subpoena, too, Ted. I must say this is a beautiful way to start the New Year—pushing something like this in your face before your eyes are even wide open. My mother and father don't know what to make of it, but I told them it's all their fault for letting me associate with bad companions. What do you think they want, anyway?"

"They want to know if I withheld the film from the court hearing on Friday morning, I suppose," Ted answered.

"Don't count on it, Ted. It looks to me like we're in deeper water than that. You aren't forgetting those letters, are you? I'll bet the prosecution's got its wind up about those. If we testify that those letters were on the film, Mr. Prentice will simply deny it. What had we better do?"

"Tell the truth. What else can we do?"

"Well, how long does it take to tell the truth? We aren't going back to college on Tuesday, that's certain. Maybe you can afford to miss some college, but if I lose a week I may never catch up again. I thought the law looked upon us as infants. How young do you have to be before you can ignore a subpoena?"

"A good deal younger than we are, I'm afraid. Sorry I got you into this mess, Nel."

"Oh, you didn't get me into anything. I went into everything with my eyes open, and if they weren't, they ought to be by this time. Well, I'm not going to sit stewing around the house all day, that's for sure. What do you feel like doing?"

"Helen Howland asked for some help this afternoon in returning those scavenger hunt things. I don't imagine she'll want that scarecrow on her front porch for very long."

"I don't mean that. Isn't there something we can do to help clear up this mess we're in?"

"About the only thing I can think of is to take that picture out to Jerry Speck to see if he recognizes the scavenger as one of the rioters."

"That doesn't sound like a very promising lead, but if it's the best we've got, then it's the best we've got. I'll see you after lunch, Ted. I'm going to try to get some more sleep, but I know I won't make it."

When Nelson appeared they drove over to Helen's and found her glad of their help. They took all the items still waiting to be returned, and loaded the scarecrow in the back seat as well. Returning the borrowed items kept them busy for an hour and a half, and then they headed for the open countryside.

"What are we going to do with this scarecrow?" asked Ted.

"Dump him somewhere alongside the road, I suppose. I'd like to get a picture of him, though."

"In winter? Wouldn't he look better in a cornfield with crows perched on his outstretched arms?"

"No, that's too commonplace. Here I've got a scarecrow in the middle of winter, forlorn and dejected because he hasn't any corn to protect or any crows to scare away. Furthermore, his stuffing is coming out of him. There's a trace of snow on the ground. If we can find the right place we can make it look like a great big heap."

They eventually found a suitable spot. Nelson pulled the scarecrow out of the car, and with Ted's help erected him near an old crisscross log fence. He made several exposures. They stood and studied their inanimate friend for a minute or two longer.

"What do you think of scarecrows, Ted? Do they really scare the crows away?"

"I doubt it. Most farms have only one scarecrow, so it must be a sort of tradition. I think crows are too smart to be fooled like that."

"I heard one farmer tell how the crows never paid any attention to him as long as he wasn't carrying his shotgun, but as soon as he came outside with the gun they all flew away. I've heard that they post sentinels while they feed, and they've got a system of warning signals. I guess a straw man like this wouldn't fool them for long."

"Crows are supposed to be pretty intelligent. A crow can learn to talk almost as well as a parrot. Do you want to leave him here?"

"Why not? He's sort of picturesque, don't you think? I mean, it's not like throwing rubbish at the side of the road. What are you doing, Ted?"

"Oh, I'm just going through the pockets of the suit, but I don't see anything. Hey, wait a minute. Here's something."

He drew out an old-fashioned watch chain from the scarecrow's pocket. "Well, how do you like that?" he exclaimed. "Then Margaret and I *did* bring back a watch chain. If we'd only known it last night, we would have won the prize."

Nelson stopped to take more pictures along the way to Echo. He had the picture of the riot with him, and was ready to produce it as they drove into the yard of Jerry's home. Both Jerry and his father were there.

Nelson merely said he wondered if Jerry could identify anyone in a picture he had with him and handed it to the boy. Jerry studied it for some moments before shaking his head.

"No, I don't know anybody there."

"What about this man here?" Nelson indicated the one with the raised shoulder. "Does he look like anybody you know?"

Again Jerry studied the picture from several angles before shaking his head again.

"No, I don't know him."

"You're sure about that, Jerry?"

"I'm pretty sure."

"Think about it carefully. Doesn't he look just like somebody you used to know?"

Jerry shook his head more violently, and his father intervened. "Who is this man that he is supposed to recognize?"

"Well, it was just a little hunch of ours. I suppose it was silly, but it seemed to us that this man looks very much like the scavenger we met out here."

"The scavenger!" Jerry exclaimed, before studying the picture again. But he ended up by shaking his head in the same manner. "No, that doesn't look anything like the scavenger."

Mr. Speck also studied the picture. "Of course I haven't seen the scavenger as many times as Jerry has, and this picture isn't very clear. But I'd have to go along with Jerry. I can't see any resemblance at all between the scavenger and the man in this picture. The scavenger seemed older than this, and heavier, too. He had white hair."

"Do you have any idea where the scavenger may have gone, Jerry?" asked Nelson.

"He told me he'd like to go to a millionaire's hotel. That's how I was sure he had a million dollars."

His father broke in a little sharply: "I didn't know you had talked to the scavenger that much, Jerry."

"Oh, he liked to talk to me whenever I was there."

The conversation continued for several minutes longer, but Mr. Speck and Jerry both refused to change their minds about the man in the picture. The boys finally thanked them and left.

"What about it, Ted?" Nelson questioned. "That man looks like the scavenger to you and to me, but not to Mr. Speck and Jerry. You don't think somebody got to them with a bribe, do you?"

Ted shook his head. "No, I think they were both being completely honest. Anyway, Jerry isn't old enough to lie as convincingly as that, after the way you questioned him."

"Then what is the matter, Ted? Are we wrong?"

"Maybe we are. That's easily possible, I suppose, since we didn't know the scavenger as well as they did. But it is possible that we are talking about two different men."

Nelson drove on in silence for a mile or two. Though Ted did not speak, the same phrase kept returning to his mind: "Two different men."

Finally he said it out loud, and Nelson flashed a quick glance at him. "You just mumbling, Ted, or do you mean something with that?"

"I don't know. I can't quite make up my mind if it means anything or not. But couldn't there be two scavengers? Jerry and his father are talking about Scavenger No. 1. We are talking about Scavenger No. 2. No wonder we can't agree. The hair ought to settle it. The man we saw certainly didn't have white hair—unless he dyed it."

"I don't get it, Ted. If you and I met Scavenger No. 2, then what happened to Scavenger No. 1?"

"He was never there in the shack."

"But it was his shack, wasn't it? Jerry pointed it out to us. There couldn't have been two different shacks."

"No, I don't think there were two shacks. They lived in the same shack, but not at the same time. Scavenger No. 1 had been there a long time, and was the one Mr. Speck and Jerry knew. But along came Scavenger No. 2, bought him out, and moved into the shack. Then we talked with him, and he returned the film to us. After that he disappeared. But the Specks probably never knew Scavenger No. 2 at all."

"Then who is this Scavenger No. 2? Do you think he's the man in the picture?"

"He could be, very easily. And I'm beginning to think his only reason for being in that shack was to return the microfilm to us."

"Why would he do that, Ted, since he was a union man? That film would hurt the union, wouldn't it?"

"Maybe he didn't know that. Maybe there's a feud between different factions of the union. It could be that the film was never in Mr. Prentice's car at all, and was never lost. The first time it appeared was when the scavenger handed it to us."

"Something's wrong, Ted. I don't believe all that. I wish we could reach the scavenger and find out the real truth. But say, which scavenger are we looking for, Scavenger No. 1 or No. 2?"

"No. 2 is our man. He was the one who returned the film. But I'm afraid he's just evaporated into thin air. We aren't going to find him. But if we could find Scavenger No. 1, he might be able to give us some information to help us."

"Find him? Are you kidding, Ted? Where would you start looking?"

"Well, let's begin by supposing that he really is exactly what he seemed to be—a scavenger. I don't know how much money he had, but I have my doubts that it was very much, or if it was, he was probably frugal with it. Then along came Scavenger No. 2. He must have given No. 1 quite a sum of money when he bought him out. So Scavenger No. 1 packed up and left. The question is, where did he go?"

"That's what I'd like to know."

"Well, what would you do if you came into an unexpected sum of money?"

"I expect I'd splurge with it."

"Maybe that's what he did, too."

"I don't know about that, Ted. If he was the miserly type, he wouldn't do that at all."

"But maybe he wasn't. Well, it was just a thought. Even if he were going to spend it, how do we know where? He told Jerry he'd like to go to a millionaire's hotel, but there are plenty of places like that if that's what he wanted."

"Not so many around here, Ted."

"Why does it have to be around here?"

"Because we don't know how much money Scavenger No. 2 gave him, but it might not have been *that* much. And your money goes a lot further when you spend it near home."

Ted thought it over. "I suppose it's just possible. It wouldn't be in Echo, of course, because No. 2 would have made him promise to leave. How about Stanton?"

"Too far and not enough glamor," Nelson surmised. "I think we can do better than that. How about Eden Park? Remember No. 2 mentioned the shack wasn't Eden Park, so there must have been some reason he thought of that hotel."

Ted slapped his fist into his palm. "Say, I'll bet that's it. That's a kind of hotel for retired wealthy people who don't particularly mind the winter weather around here. Want to give it a try?"

"Sure, why not? We're probably all wet, but we don't have anything better to do. And it's not too far from here."

Nelson turned off at the next crossroads, and headed toward Eden Park. A half hour's drive brought them to the magnificent resort. There were some pretentious buildings and large, well-kept grounds. It was an ideal place to retire if what you wanted was isolation and a variable climate—and if you had enough money.

They walked into the lobby, and Nelson stepped back to allow Ted to do the talking. He felt this was going to be a job that would require all Ted's tact and skill. If they had had the scavenger's name—and if he were still using the same name—their job might have been considerably easier.

"I'm trying to locate a gentleman who checked in here a few days ago. I'm sorry that I don't know his name, but he came from near Echo. He is an elderly man, a little heavy, with white hair."

"Oh, you must mean Mr. Weber," said the clerk in recognition. "Are you friends of his?"

"Not personally, but we are acquainted with some persons that he knows."

"I'll ring his room and ask if he will see you. Your names?"

"I'm afraid he won't recognize them, but I'm Ted Wilford, and this is Nelson Morgan."

The clerk put through the call, and then announced to them: "He says to come up. Suite 3 on the parlor floor."

The boys went up on the elevator, and soon found Mr. Weber's room. He certainly matched the description Mr. Speck had given. He greeted them as though they were old friends.

"Can I do anything for you young men? Just say the word and I'll call the room clerk and have him send up a chicken dinner."

"Oh, no, thank you," Ted protested. "We're really not hungry."

"Steak then? Some misguided souls prefer that to chicken."

"No, really, nothing at all."

"Well, then, at least sit down and make yourselves comfortable. What can I do for you?"

Ted felt a little embarrassed as to how to begin. At last he blurted out: "We're trying to locate a man who originally worked as a scavenger in the dump near Echo. Do you know anything about him?"

"Of course I do," said Mr. Weber, unabashed. "That's me."

"You're the scavenger?"

"Naturally. I explained it to them when I registered here, but they thought I was joking."

Ted felt flabbergasted by such frankness. "But isn't it rather unusual for a scavenger to live in surroundings like this?" He indicated the luxurious room around them.

"I suppose it is. I said I *was* a scavenger. I'm not a scavenger now. I came into a little money, and so I'm enjoying it. Is there anything wrong with that?"

"Would you mind telling me where your money came from?"

"Not at all. I inherited it."

"Well, I'm glad to hear of your good fortune, but we were given a different picture of the matter. Our understanding was that your place was taken by another scavenger, and that he was the one who provided you with the money for this."

"Now that just might be true. I'm a little bit scatterbrained sometimes. Suppose it did happen that way. What about it?"

"Didn't it occur to you to wonder why he gave you such a large sum of money?"

"It wasn't such a large sum. It was just enough to keep me here for a week. After that they told me I could go back to being a scavenger again. Meanwhile I'm living like a king. That's what every man wants, but few of them get it. I was given a chance to get it for one week. Why shouldn't I take it?"

"Did you ask them why they wanted you out of the way?"

"No. If there's one thing I've learned it's not to ask unnecessary questions."

"What if they were planning something illegal?"

"Then that was all the more reason why I don't want to know anything about it. The way things stand, I haven't done anything wrong."

"They didn't tell you what they wanted?"

"No, just to borrow my shack for a week, and they'd pay my board here and fit me up with new duds. Sure you won't change your minds about that chicken dinner? It's all on the bill."

"No, thank you. Did you know who these people were?"

"There was just one of them I talked to. I never saw him before, and don't expect to again. I feel quite sure about that."

"And we do, too," said Ted, smiling in spite of himself. "Are you sure they'll pay your bill here?"

"They paid it in advance. And if I happen to run over, whose fault is that? I told them I was just a scavenger."

Ted and Nelson thanked him and left. Outside, Nelson shook his head almost admiringly.

"Kind of a refreshing old codger, wasn't he? Everybody seems to be playing a role of some sort except him. He's telling everybody exactly what he is, and enjoying himself, and running up a huge bill. I like him."

"Maybe I do, too," Ted agreed. "But that's not going to help us any at the court hearing tomorrow morning."

"No," said Nelson gloomily. "Tomorrow is going to be another of my bad days."

CHAPTER 15

TED'S TESTIMONY

JUDGE HARDER RAPPED HIS GAVEL TUESDAY morning, opening the court case. He began by addressing Mr. Waring.

"Does the defense have in court the records which we requested?"

"We have, Your Honor. Here is the microfilm, and I have a projector and screen set up. We do not require absolute darkness, but if the top lights were turned off, the view would be better."

Then the judge addressed the prosecuting attorney, Mr. Davis: "Is the prosecution ready to proceed?"

"We are, Your Honor. We have not yet had a chance to examine this film, of course, but we believe it will verify other information which we propose to bring out. But first, I feel it is of the utmost importance to bring before this court the precise circumstances under which this microfilm was turned in. I should therefore like to call Ted Wilford as my first witness."

A little surprised that he should have been called first, Ted advanced to the witness chair and was sworn in. Personal information was elicited, and then Mr. Davis asked:

"Ted, is it true that you were the person who turned this film over to Mr. Waring?"

"Yes, it is."

"You turned it over to him personally; that is, you handed it directly to him with no third party intervening?"

"Yes."

"When and where did you do so?"

"Last Saturday morning about eleven o'clock in his office."

"Now, Ted, will you explain to this court exactly how this microfilm came to be in your possession? When did you first see it?"

"Last Friday evening. It must have been around six o'clock, or possibly a little later."

"And where did this happen?"

"In a little shack near a dump, just off the main road a few miles past Echo on the way to Forestdale."

"Who else was present at the time?"

"A friend of mine, Nelson Morgan, drove me out. He was there. Also the man I got the film from."

"Who was this man?"

"I don't know his name. He was a dump-picker, called a scavenger. He was living in the shack."

"How did you happen to go out to this scavenger's shack?"

Ted wondered if he ought to volunteer the information that the scavenger he had talked to wasn't the real scavenger, but he knew a witness should not volunteer information on the witness stand. His duty was to confine himself strictly to answering questions. If it should later appear that some important point had not been brought out, he could speak to one of the attorneys privately. Anyway, the identity of the scavenger was not the important point of Ted's testimony. The big thing was the letters he had seen on the film, and that Mr. Waring had later, apparently, cut out.

"Well, earlier the previous day, on Thursday, Mr. Prentice's car had run off the hill, and the film was lost from the door pocket—"

"Just a moment, Ted. I see that the defense attorney is not going to object to that answer, but I want to make the situation perfectly clear. You do not know personally that the film was in the pocket, do you?"

"No, I guess not."

"All right, then. You were told by Mr. Prentice that the film was lost from the pocket at the time of the accident. What led you to go to the scavenger's shack?"

"It wasn't Mr. Prentice who told me the film was lost. It was Mr. Waring, who telephoned me later that evening. He explained about the film, and asked if I would care to drive back to the scene of the accident and see if I could find it. My friend and I did so, but could not find the film. Then a boy passing by, by the name of Jerry Speck, told us he had seen the scavenger prowling about the wrecked car. Jerry directed us to the scavenger's shack, but when we got there the hut was dark, and there was no answer to our knock, so we left. Then Friday afternoon, after work, we drove out again. This time the scavenger was home. We asked him if he had the film, he said he did, and gave it to us."

"Now, Ted, you obviously are not in a position to testify about what happened to the film from the time it left the photographer's until it reached this courtroom. But I do want your help in identifying it to make sure this film is the same one given to you by the scavenger. First I will show you the container. Examine it carefully and state whether this is the container in which the film came."

Ted looked the container over with careful deliberation, then replied: "This is just like the container that the microfilm was in. I can't say for certain that this is the same container."

"So much for the container. Now while this film was in your possession, did you open the container and examine the film itself?"

"Yes, I did," said Ted miserably, wishing now that he had never done it.

"How did you examine it?"

"My friend and I borrowed a projector and a screen from a local photographer. Then we ran off part of the film."

"Where did this take place?"

"In the living room of my home."

"Was anyone else present?"

"No, just my friend and I."

"How much of the film did you examine?"

"That would be hard to say. I think we ran through about a third of it. But some of it we just flipped through rapidly, and some of it we stopped to read closely."

"Just so. Let's have the top lights out now, and start the film rolling. There are the first few frames, Ted. Does this look like the same film you examined in your home?"

"Yes, it does."

"All right, Ted. We are going to continue running this film. If at any time we go too fast, I want you to tell us to stop the film. The question I want you to answer is whether or not you notice anything different about this film than when you previously examined it."

That was the question Ted was anxious to have answered, too, but he was afraid he already knew the answer. That last telephone call from Mr. Waring had given him the idea. He felt sure that Mr. Waring and Mr. Prentice had doctored the film—cut out the incriminating letters. Mr. Davis must also have some inkling of what had happened, and that was the purpose of his questions to Ted.

"Are we going too fast, Ted?" he asked.

"No, this is the part we just flipped through. I wouldn't be able to tell for sure whether it is the same or not."

"But you haven't noticed anything that looks different so far?"

"No, not yet."

Then they came to the end of the long bookkeeping section. Ted asked that the film be slowed down, and this was done. But the letters did not appear. To make sure, Ted let the film go on a bit longer without saying anything. At last he was certain that the letters had been cut out.

"I'm not sure," he volunteered at last, "but I think there are some letters that ought to have been in there."

"Where was that, Ted?"

"A minute or so back. They should have showed up, but they haven't."

"All right, Ted. We'll reverse the film. When we come to the part where you think the letters belong please tell us."

The film was reversed and run back quite some distance, then started forward again. At last Ted said:

"I think it was right here."

"Where, Ted? I want you to locate the spot just as accurately as you can."

At Ted's direction the film was shifted slowly back and forth, until he said:

"That's it, as accurately as I can place it."

"Very well. May I ask you, Ted, if you know anything about film splicing?"

"Yes."

"Do you know why a film is spliced?"

"Sometimes it accidentally breaks and has to be glued back together."

"Can you think of any other reason?"

"I suppose if you wanted to cut something out of a film, you would have to splice it together again when you were finished."

"Just so. Do you think you would recognize a splice when you saw it?"

"Yes, I think so."

"Then let's have the top lights on again, and I want the witness to examine the film to determine whether there is a splice at the point where he has indicated."

Ted left the stand as the lights went on, and walked over to the projector to examine the film. He had no trouble at all locating the splice. It was right where he had expected it.

"It's here," he announced.

"Then please take your seat again. Would you say that that splice, coming exactly at the point where you expected to find several letters, would indicate that something had been cut out of this film?"

"Objection!" Mr. Waring called. "That calls for a conclusion from the witness. The film may have been accidentally broken."

"You've made your point, Mr. Davis," the judge ruled. "Please continue with the witness."

"Ted, you say that you saw several letters on this film last week that are not there now. How many letters do you refer to?"

"There were three of them."

"I want you to describe those letters, Ted, just as accurately as you can."

Mr. Waring was on his feet again. "I object, Your Honor. Since the letters are not here in this court, we are unable to examine them for authenticity, and therefore I believe no testimony should be admitted concerning them. This borders on hearsay."

"Your Honor," said Mr. Davis smoothly, "it is not *our* fault that the letters are not here."

"This court is anxious to get to the bottom of this affair," Judge Harder ruled. "I am going to admit this testimony for the time being."

"I'll ask you again to describe those letters, Ted," Mr. Davis continued.

"The first two letters were addressed to Mr. Channing Noble, and they were signed by Mr. Jed Myers. The first letter asked for an appointment. The second letter thanked him for the appointment, and said he would accept the percentages. The third letter was written to Mr. Jed Myers, and signed by Mr. Channing Noble. It said he was glad they had been able to arrive at an agreement, and that he was looking forward to a long and satisfactory relationship."

There was a buzz in the courtroom, stifled by the judge's gavel.

"On what sort of paper was this third letter written?"

"Well, it had the name and address of the union across the top."

"I show you one of the union's letterheads. Was it on paper like this?"

"Yes, it was."

"This reference to percentages—what did you understand it to mean in the context given?"

"Objection!" said Mr. Waring, rising. "That is an improper question, and calls for a conclusion of the witness."

"I withdraw the question, Your Honor. Just one more point, Ted. From the time that you saw these letters with the projector until you delivered the film to Mr. Waring, was this film ever out of your possession?"

"No, it was not."

"Isn't it a fact that you were aware of its importance, and that you exercised great caution to safeguard it?"

"Yes, that is true."

"That's all." Mr. Davis walked away and sat down. "Your witness."

Mr. Waring came forward. "Ted, you work part time as a newspaper reporter. That type of work teaches you to be very accurate, does it not?"

"We try to be accurate," Ted agreed.

"At the same time, you are an imaginative person, Ted, are you not?"

"I don't quite know what you mean."

"You've also done some creative writing apart from your newspaper work. Is it true that while a senior in high school you won a prize for a story in a scholastic magazine?"

"Yes, I did."

"And is it also true that at college you have had a story accepted for the school's magazine which is a rare honor for a freshman?"

"Yes, I guess that's so."

"I think this indicates, Ted, that you are an imaginative person, and I want to suggest to you that these letters you have described to this court are entirely the product of your undoubtedly very active imagination."

"No, that is not true at all," said Ted.

"You say these three letters were on the film when you gave it to me. But you didn't see them this morning, did you?"

"No."

"And in fact they are not on that film now."

"No—not unless I happened to miss them."

"No, you didn't miss them, Ted. I have gone over the film very carefully, and those letters are not there now." Mr. Waring leaned forward grimly. "What would you say, Ted, if I were to tell you that I have four witnesses who will state that the letters you described were never on that film at all?"

Before Ted could answer, Judge Harder rapped his gavel loudly for attention.

"This is a very serious charge, Mr. Waring. Is it true that you do have four witnesses to this fact?"

"Yes, Your Honor," said Mr. Waring, turning toward the bench. "I, of course, am one of the witnesses. But my secretary and another employee can testify that after I received that film from Ted, it was locked away in my safe, before I could possibly have had the opportunity to tamper with it. Later that day, both these persons, as well as Mr. Prentice, were present when the film was removed from the safe. We were all there when the film was projected in my office, and all four of us will swear that those letters were not on it."

"Could the film have been tampered with when it was supposedly in the safe?"

"No, Your Honor. My employees were in the office all that time."

Judge Harder turned to Ted with a very serious expression. "Ted, you have stated that you are eighteen years old and that you are a college student. This would indicate that you must have some familiarity with legal procedures. Nevertheless, you may not be fully cognizant of your privileges and duties as a witness. Are you aware of the serious penalties which may accrue to you if you are found guilty of perjury?"

"Yes, Your Honor, I am," said Ted, wishing he could sink through the floor.

"Did it occur to you to consult with an attorney before you testified this morning?"

"No," Ted answered wretchedly, "I didn't think I needed a lawyer. I did talk with Mr. Waring a few times."

"But Mr. Waring did not undertake to represent you?"

"No."

"And is that your understanding, too, Mr. Waring?"

"Yes, Your Honor. I considered the witness to be friendly to our cause, and his testimony this morning came as a complete surprise to me. Naturally, I could not undertake to represent him now, since it appears that his interests are contrary to those of my client."

"Mr. Waring, this court is not going to allow this cross-examination to continue. We have a special duty to protect the welfare of minor persons who come before it, and it appears that this witness has not availed himself of the legal assistance to which he is entitled, nor did he, apparently, receive any instructions from you to do so."

"Your Honor, if I am not to have the privilege of cross-examination, then I move that this witness' entire testimony be stricken from the record."

"Your motion is denied, with the stipulation that the witness may be recalled at a later time for re-examination, on condition that he has been provided with legal counsel. Apparently he has relied upon your advice up until this time. I instruct you to give him any assistance he may need in procuring adequate counsel. The witness is dismissed and his present subpoena nullified."

Ted left the stand and walked through to the back of the courtroom, where Nelson was sitting.

"I'm going," he whispered hoarsely. "This is enough for me."

"What about my subpoena?"

"I don't think they'll want you, for they would have the same difficulty with your testimony as they did with mine. Maybe you can get Mr. Davis to dismiss it for you."

There was a temporary lull in proceedings, and Nelson was able to get the attention of Mr. Davis, who agreed to withdraw the subpoena. The two boys left the courtroom together.

CHAPTER 16

TED'S PERJURY

"THEY'RE ALL A BUNCH OF CROOKS!" TED RAGED outside. "The four of them are all in it together—Mr. Waring, Mr. Prentice, the secretary, and his other employee, whoever that is. I'll bet everybody in the courtroom thought I was lying. Well, that's what I get for sticking my neck out. I thought those people who denied they saw the milk truck overturned were being cowardly, but now I think they were just being smart. Why get mixed up in anything you don't have to? The crooks will always lie to back each other up, and that makes you look wrong."

"Boy, you've sure got it bad," said Nelson, nodding his head in sympathy. "I understand how you feel, though. I could just as easily have been the person up there on the witness stand. I didn't have the film in my possession the way you did, but I did see those letters. I suppose they decided to call you first on account of Jim Horner's story in the paper. Did you see him in the courtroom this morning? He just might take your side of it, and write his story so the union will look bad. And of course most of his readers will believe whatever he says."

"I don't care what he writes," Ted answered somberly. "I'd just like to wash my hands of the whole ugly business."

"How'd you like to start back to college—right now?" Nelson suggested suddenly. "What's to stop us? I'm about packed, and I'll bet you are, too. If we start right after lunch we can still make it tonight, even though we'd have to drive after dark for a few hours. Then we won't miss any college. After all, college is our business—not this rotten mess. And with those subpoenas canceled, there's no reason why we can't."

Ted thought it over for a moment. The prospect was enticing, but he finally shook his head. "No, I guess not. It's all right to say we'd like to wash our hands of it, but if a bad strike develops, can you really say it doesn't mean anything to you, just because you're away? Besides, I've had a bad write-up in the paper, I've been accused of perjury, and Mr. Waring may want to issue a new subpoena for me. How can I run away from all that?"

"No, I guess you can't," Nelson agreed. "But how long does that mean you have to wait?"

"For the rest of today, anyway, I suppose. By that time Mr. Waring can issue his subpoena if he wants to. Maybe something else will turn up at the hearing today. I guess I ought to have stayed, but I thought they'd probably put those people on the stand to say I was lying, and I just didn't feel like taking any more of that today."

"Isn't it important to know what they're saying about you?"

"Oh, I'll know, all right. Things like that don't stay secret. And if I do have to go back to court, I'll have a lawyer, and you can bet he'll go over all the testimony in detail. I suppose I ought to call Mr. Dobson and let him know what happened. He didn't ask me to cover the story, because he thought I'd be on my way to college. Anyway, Carl Allison will be back this afternoon, and he'll be able to pick up the story."

"We can stop at the *Town Crier* office almost as easily as telephone," Nelson pointed out.

"No, I'd rather telephone. I don't feel like meeting anybody, not even Mr. Dobson. Let's go to my house. We can pick up our lunch there, and we can gripe to our hearts' content. What do you think of two men—Mr. Waring and Mr. Prentice—who would tamper with that film and then accuse me of lying?"

"Pretty shabby, after the way we tried to help them. I don't think they would have done it unless they felt it was very important. You know, Ted, you may have caught them off guard. Mr. Waring said your testimony came as a surprise, and I believe him. They had no idea we had looked at the film, and when you testified the way you did, they didn't know what to do."

"So they lied—and I'm the one accused of lying," said Ted bitterly.

He put through his call to Mr. Dobson, and the editor listened very attentively.

"I'm not going to ask if you are telling the truth, Ted, because I know you are. But I wouldn't feel too bad about things. The truth has a way of coming out, and you can be sure if there's any way the resources of this newspaper can be used to bring it out, I'll do it. The important thing at the moment is whether you feel you need an attorney. If you do, I'll arrange it for you."

"No, I don't think so, Mr. Dobson—not unless I get another subpoena. I guess the damage has been done already. But thanks very much for suggesting it."

"What are your plans now, Ted?"

"I'm going to leave for college early tomorrow morning—if the law lets me."

"Fine, Ted. And if you do, try not to worry about things. I'll do the best I can for you here. The people who really matter, the people who know you and believe in you, aren't going to believe wild accusations like this."

Ted felt a little better as he hung up the phone. "He's standing by me," he announced. "Of course I knew he would. And you've been standing by, too, but maybe I'm being selfish. There isn't any reason why you shouldn't go back to college without me."

"Nothing doing, Ted. We're in this thing together. I'll wait till morning. I don't think one day will kill me."

"What if I get a subpoena?"

"Then I'll probably get one, too."

"You could avoid it by leaving today."

"No, I don't think I want to—not after the brave thing you did today."

"Me? Brave?" asked Ted in surprise.

"Why, sure. What do you think? How many people would get up on the witness stand and talk the way you did today?"

"I just told the truth. What else could I do?"

"But there are plenty of people who would hesitate about telling the truth where Jed Myers is concerned."

"Jed Myers? I didn't look at it that way. I felt all I was doing was testifying against the union. Jed Myers is in prison already, and I can't hurt his associates still on the outside. I don't see anything brave about that."

"O.K., Ted, but it is anyway. If you're going to be like that, then the least I can do is stick by you. What would you like to do this afternoon?"

"I know what I'd *like* to do—go out and ride and ride, so far away that nobody could find us."

"Especially a process server," Nelson grinned. "But I thought that was the whole purpose in staying in town today—so that we *won't* be dodging a subpoena. I've got that roll of film I took yesterday and developed last night. I'd like to print some pictures before I leave town. Want to help me?"

"I don't mind helping you, but I'd rather not talk to anybody today."

"We'll be alone in my basement. This is a school day for the kids, remember? And maybe you could even drill me a little on history during some of the pauses."

Though they took a history book to Nelson's basement with them, they didn't get very far with it. Nelson was more interested in his photography, which was somewhat exacting, since he was making enlargements, and Ted could not help brooding over the affairs of the morning.

"Want to give me a hand with this, Ted? This scarecrow turned out pretty well, and I want to blow it up as large as I can."

Ted cooperated with him, until eventually they had enough prints of everything to satisfy even Nelson. Ted wondered what he was going to do with all these copies.

"This is going to be my contest winner," Nelson informed him confidently as he looked at the scarecrow picture.

"In black-and-white? I thought color was the thing nowadays."

"Oh, there's still quite a market for black-and-white. Anyway, these gray tones seem more typical of a wintry day. Besides, they've got a process now for bringing all the natural colors out of black-and-white negatives."

"You're kidding."

"No, I'm not. Nobody understands how it works, but they just know it does."

They discussed this and other things while waiting for the prints to dry. As they talked, inevitably the conversation returned to the morning's affair.

"I think it was pretty nice of Judge Harder not to let you go on without an attorney, Ted. There are more booby traps in the law than you can shake a stick at. I know you were telling the truth as well as you could, but an attorney could have warned you that you said something that wasn't quite true."

"What was that? I tried to be as careful as I could, because I know how much that means in court."

"Well, you said that the microfilm was never out of your possession, from the time we ran it on the projector until you turned it over to Mr. Waring."

"Wasn't that true? I even slept with it under my pillow, and carried it in my pocket the rest of the time."

"Not *all* the time. It was locked up in the glove compartment of my car while we were investigating the trouble on Post Haste Road."

"That's the same thing, isn't it? Nobody tampered with your car, did they?"

"Not so far as I know."

"They would have had to unlock the car door, and the door to the glove compartment, and we weren't out of sight of the car for very long. You didn't see any signs of tampering, did you?"

"No, and you usually do when sneak thieves are at work. You're right about the time, too. I don't think an ordinary sneak thief would have had time for it. But remember we may not be dealing with ordinary thieves. There's a good chance we're mixed up with Jed Myers and his mob."

Ted felt almost stunned. "Say, that might be true, at that. If we're going to regard those letters as authentic, then there was some sort of connection between the union and Jed Myers. You think a professional could have broken into your car and the glove compartment so quickly, without leaving any traces?"

"Sure, easily. Those locks aren't that complex."

"But what about the microfilm? It was still in the glove compartment. There wouldn't have been time to cut out those letters and splice the film together again."

"No, but they might have had a substitute film all ready, without the letters on it. You know something? That whole trouble out on Post Haste Road—maybe the only purpose of it was to get you out there so they could try to get the film away from you."

Ted considered seriously. "No, I don't think that was the *only* reason, but it might have been *one* of the reasons. Someone was careful to report the matter to the *Town Crier,* and it was a nine-out-of-ten chance that I'd be sent out there. I've thought of something else. That last man we saw—the one who came walking up—*he* may have been the one who changed the films. Then he gave them the signal that he had found it, and they let us go, and left soon after."

"Could be," Nelson agreed. "I thought it was kind of funny they didn't search us to see if we had any more film. But they didn't have to. It wasn't the camera film they were after. They were after the microfilm in the car. After they had found that, they didn't need us any more. But if they *hadn't* found it, then they would have searched us."

Ted shook his head savagely. "If this is true, then I really did commit perjury this morning, without meaning to. And Mr. Prentice and Mr. Waring must think I'm lying just the way I thought they were. No wonder they were bitter about me."

"But it's just supposition so far," Nelson cautioned. "We still don't have any real proof."

"No. But maybe our thinking has been too narrow. We've been thinking that Mr. Prentice and Mr. Waring and their two witnesses are lying. Let's imagine they're telling the truth, and then see where that leaves us. I can think of one thing that was bothering me. How come there was a splice in that film, right at the point where the letters were supposed to be missing?"

"They had to splice it, after they cut out the letters."

"Sure. But you told me yourself that it would be possible to make a new print of the film, so the splice wouldn't show."

"Maybe there wasn't time."

"If Mr. Prentice and Mr. Waring cut out the letters, that must have been on Saturday afternoon. They had from Saturday night till Tuesday morning to get a new print made. Of course they might reason that the splice probably wouldn't be found, but would they really take a chance on that, on a matter as important as this one? It makes more sense to believe that the films were exchanged in the glove compartment, and that the new film was deliberately spliced to make it look as though something had been cut out."

"All right, Ted. You might have something here. But let's go easy. This whole thing still doesn't make sense."

"No, it doesn't," Ted agreed. "But remember it doesn't make much sense the other way, either. Suppose Mr. Prentice and Mr. Waring cut out the letters. All right, we can understand why they did that. But it leaves a good many other things that we can't understand. Who drove Mr. Prentice's car off the road, and how did Scavenger No. 2 happen to be right there on the spot? Who is Scavenger No. 2 anyway, and what finally happened to him? We're pretty sure that he was present at the scene of the riot on Saturday morning, so he wasn't just out in that shack for his *own* purposes. He was tied in with someone else. We thought he must be tied in with the union, because we thought it was the union that was doing the rioting. But maybe it wasn't the union at all. It's more likely that he was tied in with Jed Myers's mob, and they are the ones who were rioting."

"Remember Jim Horner?" Nelson's voice, like Ted's, was getting excited. "We know that someone has been feeding him information—enough of it true so that he thought all of it was true. But his stories have been unfavorable to the union, so it wasn't the union that was doing it."

"But is all this beginning to make any kind of sense?" asked Ted wonderingly. "Why? What's back of everything?"

"If someone was trying to discredit the union, give it unfavorable publicity, stir up a strike—then it all begins to make some sort of sense, doesn't it?"

"Yes, maybe it does, and maybe that's the only way that it *can* make sense. All right, let's start all over. Let's suppose that Mr. Prentice is telling the truth. Suppose he did have that microfilm in the door pocket of his car, and the film did not have those incriminating letters on it. Then someone ran his car off the road, at a spot that had been agreed upon in advance. Maybe they wanted to kill him, maybe they didn't. Maybe they simply wanted to get that film and didn't care how they did it. The scavenger was waiting on the spot where he had been stationed. This wasn't the original scavenger, whom they had bought out and sent away, a temporarily happy man. Jerry Speck actually saw Scavenger No. 2 at the scene of the wreck, but thought it was Scavenger No. 1, because he only saw him from a distance. He probably thought he recognized him from the sort of clothes he was wearing, what he was doing, and the direction he took when he left. The second scavenger had been very careful to avoid a chance meeting with Jerry, or anyone else. He was substituted at the last possible moment, and of course he disappeared as soon as his mission was accomplished.

"Scavenger No. 2 found the microfilm in the wreck, and took it with him. Since he was away from his shack that night, we can be pretty sure what he was doing. He was taking that microfilm away to be reprocessed. A copy was made and forged letters added to it, and still another copy made so that the splices wouldn't show. Since those letters were forgeries, they must have been prepared by experts. It was this last microfilm which was given to us by the scavenger, and the original microfilm was finally returned to us in the glove compartment of your car—except that a splice had been added to make it look as though something was missing."

"What was the purpose of all this, Ted?"

"They wanted to get these forged letters at least into the public eye, and possibly into the court proceedings. If they were published, a large part of the public was going to believe them. And if they were introduced into court, probably experts would testify on both sides, some claiming that the letters were authentic, and some claiming they were forgeries. Maybe the matter couldn't be settled, but once again the union was going to get a black eye."

"Then why didn't they go through with that plan, Ted?"

"Because there were certain difficulties. If possible they wanted to avoid introducing those letters into court, where it just might be possible to prove them forgeries. It would be better if they could get somebody to testify about those letters in court, without actually producing them. Since we had read the letters, we could do it. Jim Horner, who must have been tipped off about those letters somehow, found out that we *had* read them, by learning about the projector we borrowed. Mr. Davis had us subpoenaed. The job was done. Now if they could substitute the *old* microfilm again, this would make it look even worse for the union, for it would seem to prove that the union had been guilty of suppressing evidence. We did their dirty work for them—anyway I did. If not us, they probably had some other scheme in reserve."

"This is all beautiful, Ted," said Nelson with a touch of skepticism, "but where's your proof? Until you get that, it's just a pretty theory. Meanwhile, some people are going to believe that you lied in court—which apparently you did—and others that the union is rotten to the core, and the chances of heading off a disastrous strike look pretty low."

"Yes, I know," said Ted thoughtfully. "Well, I can't imagine where we're going to get the evidence to prove it tonight, and I don't think we ought to delay our return to college beyond tomorrow morning."

"Even if you haven't any proof, don't you think you ought to tell somebody what you suspect?"

"Whom should I tell? I hate to go to Mr. Waring or Mr. Prentice with this story, because we might be wrong, and then we'll find we're playing the wrong side of the fence. I suppose I'll tell Mr. Dobson, and he can put Carl Allison to work on it, if he wants to."

"And you know just how anxious Carl Allison will be to do anything for you, Ted."

"Yes, I know. Ken Kutler would be a better bet, but unfortunately he works for the wrong newspaper, and I'd feel disloyal giving him a tip instead of our paper. Well, the day isn't over yet. Maybe something will still turn up."

Nelson's pictures were about dry, and he turned them over from the drying plate. The enlarged scarecrow had come out especially good, and he was enthusiastic about it.

"Isn't that something, Ted? Doesn't he look almost human?"

"It's good," Ted agreed, but without Nelson's high enthusiasm, for his mind was still preoccupied with other things.

"I'd say it's more than good." A touch of awe had come into Nelson's voice. Even Ted caught this note at last, and looked at his friend in surprise. "Listen to me, Ted. I said he looks almost human, doesn't he?"

"And I agreed," Ted returned.

"Ted, when you look at a person, and talk to him, what do you notice most about him?"

"Why, I suppose I don't really pay very much attention to how he looks, because I'm concentrating on what he's saying, so I will be sure to quote him correctly."

"Well, with me it's different. I often don't pay any attention to what he's saying, because I'm thinking about how he looks, and what sort of picture he'd make. Now take a good look, Ted. Who does that scarecrow remind you of?"

"Mm." Ted narrowed his eyes. "It just might be Mr. Halliday. That could be an old suit of his."

"Sure, it could, and it probably is. The Boy Scouts probably asked him for permission to hold their Halloween party in his barn. They told him they were decorating a scarecrow, so he gave them one of his old suits. No, that's not what I meant. Think, Ted, think. I don't want to tell you, because you've got to see it for yourself to be sure I'm not making it up."

A look of growing understanding passed across Ted's face, followed in a moment by incredulity. "Oh, no, this is just another of your crazy ideas. Remember the trouble we got into by following up on your last one? Well, this one is even sillier."

"Then you *do* see it," Nelson persisted. "It's not just my imagination. Look at the cut of that coat—the lapels—it's an out-of-date style you don't see any more. And whoever wears a vest like that? And the cut of the trousers. I'm even sure about the color. It looks black on the picture, but it wasn't really. It was a fairly light blue. Do you see it now, Ted?"

"Yes, I see it now," Ted agreed dully, for his mind had jumped another step ahead, a step that Nelson had not yet thought of. "You mean that the scarecrow and Scavenger No. 2 were both wearing the same suit."

"It doesn't make much sense, does it?" said Nelson, still excited. "But I'm so sure of it I'd almost be ready to swear to it in court."

"It makes sense, all right," Ted went on soberly. "Suppose you came into a strange town on an assignment of some sort. You were wearing a good suit, because you didn't know exactly what your assignment was going to be. Then you were told, and you found that you needed old clothes for it. You didn't have any old clothes with you, and it isn't a simple matter to acquire old clothes in a strange town—particularly if you are anxious to keep your mission a secret. But you find this old scarecrow, so you simply appropriate his clothes till your job is done. Then you put them back on him afterward. Remember that Scavenger No. 2 had a neat haircut, even though he did let his beard grow for a day or two. That will explain about that watch chain in the pocket, too. A person finding the chain wouldn't be likely to put it in the scarecrow's pocket. But he might easily put it in his *own* pocket—that is, the pocket of the suit he was wearing at the time."

Now Nelson was beginning to get an inkling of that next step which Ted had already guessed.

"But that means Scavenger No. 2 must have made at least two visits to Mr. Halliday's barn. It was locked, but I suppose it wouldn't be a difficult task to break into it—"

"No, Nel, he wouldn't have to break in if he went there to meet someone. Mr. Halliday said he hadn't been out to the barn since Halloween, but he must have been there sometime after the scarecrow was made. I don't suppose he even knew about the scavenger's borrowing the scarecrow's clothes, or else he wouldn't have been so helpful about leading us to the scarecrow. And of course he never dreamed his watch chain was in the scarecrow's pocket—the same chain Margaret had seen just a week or two ago."

"But this is still speculation, Ted. Where are you going to get the proof you need?"

Ted rose to his feet. "I'm going to get it from the best possible source. I'm going to ask Mr. Halliday."

Nelson stared straight at his friend. "I'll go with you."

"No, I want to go alone. This is a job I have to do for myself."

\CHAPTER 17

RIDING LOW

TED'S RING WAS ANSWERED BY MR. HALLIDAY. His face showed an expression which was not so much surprised as it was relieved.

"Come in, Ted, come in."

Pausing only to kick off his rubbers, Ted followed his friend into the living room. Seating himself, Mr. Halliday motioned Ted toward a chair. But Ted did not sit down, and as he started to speak Mr. Halliday interrupted smoothly:

"Wait a minute, Ted. Let me say something first. I've reached out my hand at least half a dozen times today to call you, but each time I've hesitated. Call it cowardice if you wish, but I don't think it was that so much as the realization that I didn't know what to say to you. But I'm glad you've come now—very, very glad."

Then Mr. Halliday *did* know why he was there. Still Ted clung to a thread of hope. He took the watch chain from his pocket.

"Is this yours, Mr. Halliday? I don't have any right to question you, and you don't have to answer if you don't want to. But if you told me that it *isn't* yours, it would sure take a big load off my mind."

Mr. Halliday took the chain and examined it carefully. "It looks very much like a watch chain I used to have. Yes, I would say that it is probably mine."

"Well, where did you lose it?" Ted spoke wildly.

The elderly man managed a faint smile, which immediately disappeared. "I imagine that I lost it wherever you happened to find it. Suppose you tell me that first."

"I found it in the pocket of the scarecrow, the one we got from your barn."

"Well, no, I hardly think I could have lost it in the pocket of a scarecrow—"

"But you *did* lose it in the barn, and afterward the man wearing the scarecrow's clothes found it and put it in his pocket."

"You've explained that logically, Ted. Although I never dreamed of it till now, that was probably exactly the way it happened."

"But you told me that you hadn't been out to the barn since Halloween—"

"That was a lie, of course, Ted. As far as I know it is the first lie I ever told you, and I am going to make very sure that it is the last one. Sit down, Ted. It isn't necessary for you to ask me any more questions. I want to tell you all about it. I think you're the only person I could tell, and so I'm glad that you're the one who found me out."

He waited a moment till Ted was seated, then resumed:

"You've known me for a long time, Ted, and I flatter myself that you've held a high opinion of me. For most of my life I have been just what I appeared to be—an upright, hard-working businessman. And then I did something which fills me with shame. Well, this is my story.

"I've built up an investment company here that meant everything to me. I don't think this has been a purely selfish ambition of mine. The community needed an establishment like mine. I give employment to a dozen people, and for hundreds of other people I offer the best investment advice I can give. So you see, in one sense I felt that I own something in the nature of a public trust. It wasn't merely my own money that was involved. I had the money of hundreds of other investors to consider. That is why it was of the utmost importance to me that the company remain financially sound.

"My company did well for a long time as the market expanded. You've heard the expression 'riding high.' One piece of good fortune seems to breed another, and everything goes well for a long stretch. Unfortunately the opposite thing can also happen. Bad luck seems to breed more bad luck, and then we might say the person or business is 'riding low.' I regret to say that lately my firm has been in trouble.

"I need not go into details, except to say that we are obliged to issue a new financial statement in March. I felt it was absolutely essential if the company were not to go bankrupt that we have a better picture to present to my investors than we do now. The best way I could think of—a desperate way, but almost the only way for us—was to entice new investment money into our company. This, I thought, might be done if we could get Mr. Abbott to sell out his large trucking interests, and put some of the proceeds into our company. This would encourage other people to invest their money with us, and keep us in business.

"Mr. Abbott had complained several times about the way things were going with him. We knew he was especially disgruntled over labor relations. He felt that trying to get along with a union was like running on a treadmill—you can never keep up with them because they always demand more. He had mentioned the possibility of retiring in June. But June was a little too late for me. If I could only get him to move that date up by a few months, it would make a world of difference to me. Stirring up some labor trouble which would irritate him might hurry him up.

"I'm certainly not justifying what I did, Ted. It was a very wrong thing, and I shall regret it the rest of my life. Of course I knew that I was hurting the union, but I excused it by thinking that I would improve labor-management relations if I ever got control of the company.

"Now I'd like to try to explain about my relations with Jed Myers' associates. I wanted them to create a few minor disturbances which would be blamed on the union. I expected that they would feed a few news tips to Jim Horner—slanted, though basically true. If Horner should appear to find a connection between Jed Myers and the union, then this would help my case. I thought there might be some attempt to delay Mr. Prentice in presenting his records in court, thereby adding unfavorable publicity to the union. In view of what I was trying to accomplish, these things didn't seem so bad to me at the time. You often hire a public relations firm to help create a *good* public impression, so why not try the opposite? I want you to believe, Ted, that this is all I ever intended."

"But—" Ted objected "—you were out at the barn and met these men before the accident. You must have known then what they were planning."

"Not quite, Ted, though my suspicions were first aroused at that meeting. One of the men there was the associate I had been in contact with, and the other was an out-of-state man who had just arrived. The associate explained to us the plan for having this man take the scavenger's place. I had some misgivings, but was given to understand that it was merely intended to lure Mr. Prentice there with some sort of message and then to 'lose' his records for a short time. When I learned of the auto accident I was filled with horror—and disgust with myself. I have since learned of other things—telephoned threats, and so on. There can be no justification for things like that.

"I immediately tried to call them off—to put an end to the disturbances I had hired them to create. And then I learned something which I should have been smart enough to foresee. They had no intention of listening to me. They wanted control of the trucking industry for themselves. They didn't think they had anything to fear from me. I had already compromised myself, and they felt I could be counted on not to do anything that would expose my own role in the affair.

"But I want you to believe one thing, Ted. I never had the slightest intention of giving in to them. From that moment when I told them to stop, and they laughed at me, I knew that this whole thing would have to come out. I was simply biding my time, trying to decide the best way of doing it. You do believe me, don't you, Ted?"

"Yes, I believe you," he answered.

"Thank you, Ted. That means more to me than you can possibly know. The thing I regret above all else is the loss of your good opinion of me."

"You haven't lost that, Mr. Halliday," said Ted, shaking his head. "I can't forget everything you've done for me, just because of one thing that's happened."

"But have you really considered, Ted, what I've done to you? Because of me you've been castigated in the city paper. You have been placed in a position where many people are going to believe you committed perjury on the witness stand today. And what if you had been in the car with Mr. Prentice when it went over the hill? It was mere chance that you rode back to town with Nelson instead of with him. Can you forgive all that, Ted?"

"I don't have to forgive it, Mr. Halliday, because I can understand the strain you were under. And all those things that happened to me—you couldn't have known they would happen. If you had, you would never have done it."

Mr. Halliday turned his head to stare out the window for a few moments at the deepening twilight. "No, Ted, I know now there was a better way. I should have played fair with my investors. I should have let them know the way the situation stood. If they chose to desert me, and the company collapsed, at least we would have gone down in an honorable fashion. But all this would have hurt my pride. I didn't want people to know I'd made a series of business mistakes. It was my pride that was the ruin of me, after all."

"No," said Ted firmly, "you did it because you thought this was the best way to protect your investors."

His friend turned his head to look him squarely in the face. "Then if you still believe in me, Ted, there is one more thing you can do for me. I want you to write the story up for your paper."

Ted was stunned. "I want to help you, Mr. Halliday. I'd do anything I could for you. But I—I can't write the story."

"Why not, Ted?" he asked.

"Because—because there's been too much between us for so long. Because I know that some of the things you told me tonight are things you would never have told anyone else. It would be too much to put down on paper. Carl Allison is back in town. Let him do it. Or Ken Kutler. Or—"

"Do you think they could understand me better than you do, Ted? You're the only one who knows, and almost—I think—the only one who cares. Will you, Ted?"

Ted hesitated for a long time. "All right—if you want me to," he agreed at last.

"Thank you, Ted. It was a big thing to ask, and I wouldn't have done it if I didn't know you were big enough to do it. Only by convincing people of what really happened can you vindicate the union and help me undo the harm I've done. Let's close the book on that for now. Tell me all about college."

"Do you really care? Can that matter now?"

"Of course I care, Ted, and it matters more than you can appreciate. Have you decided to go on with your mathematics?"

"Well, I—" and Ted, surprisingly, found himself sitting there another fifteen minutes discussing his own problems, while his friend occasionally offered a few quiet words of advice.

Then Ted left, and found himself walking fast, as though, if he walked fast enough, he might leave his churning thoughts behind him.

CHAPTER 18

THE BIG STORY

IT WAS STILL QUITE EARLY IN THE MORNING when Ted went to the *Town Crier* office and laid a sheet of paper on Mr. Dobson's desk.

"Here's your story, Mr. Dobson," he said briefly.

"Have you talked with Mr. Waring?"

"Yes. He thanked me, and said he wouldn't need me in court again. And he said Jim Horner is going to print a retraction."

The editor did not look at the paper but instead kept his eyes on Ted. "Sit down a minute, Ted," he invited.

"Nelson's waiting out in the car," Ted explained. "We're on our way back to college."

"This won't take long."

Glancing quickly at Miss Monroe, Ted sat down on the chair but did not lean back. He wished that the editor hadn't stopped him; he wished that Miss Monroe hadn't been present.

Mr. Dobson hesitated, feeling for words. At last he gave up any attempt to remember the little speech he had prepared, and said instead:

"Ted, I thought I had something to say to you, but now I'm not sure that I do. I've no fault to find with the way you handled this story, although you yourself seem dissatisfied. Somehow it seems to you that you had to choose between your loyalty to Mr. Halliday and your loyalty to the newspaper, but I don't think that was the real problem at all."

"I wouldn't have written the story, if Mr. Halliday hadn't told me to," said Ted bitterly.

"We can't be sure, Ted, what you might have done, but if you hadn't written it, I wouldn't have blamed you. So you see, Ted, I don't think you would have been disloyal to the paper, or to Mr. Halliday, either. There's only one standard to go by: whether you did the thing that conformed to your own particular set of values. I think you did, and having done it, there's no reason for regret."

Ted stood up. "Do you want to check that story before I go?"

"No, Ted, I don't think that will be necessary. I'm sure it's accurate. You were there, and you know how it happened better than anyone else. I don't want to keep you any longer. Stop in when you get home in the spring."

"I will, Mr. Dobson. Good-by. Good-by, Miss Monroe."

"Good-by, Ted," his two friends called to him as he turned and left the office.

Out on the road Nelson seemed to gloat. "Good driving," he commented. "Better than you can expect at this time of year. We've only missed one day of college, and that's not so bad—not half as bad as I expected. That sure was a lucky thing, your finding that watch chain and recognizing the scavenger on that riot picture, and then my remembering about the scavenger's clothes."

"Lucky for whom?" said Ted caustically.

"If Mr. Halliday can prove his relations with Jed Myers were just what he told you, I don't suppose they'll put him in jail."

Ted did not answer.

"Funny about those threatening telephone calls. Mr. Abbott was willing to blame them on the union. But Mr. Prentice was receiving them all along, too, and he didn't let it bother him. He knew the owners wouldn't do stupid things like that."

"Do you have to keep talking about it?" Ted put in irritably.

"What are we supposed to do? Ride along without saying anything?"

"Well, what's wrong with a little silence for a change?"

Knowing that Ted would get over his grouch before very long, Nelson subsided for a few miles. Then he remarked casually:

"There was a lot doing this vacation, but I'll be sort of glad to get back to college. Work isn't so bad, once you buckle down to it. Mr. Dobson gave me permission to try to sell that riot picture to one of the photographic magazines, too, so maybe I'm not too far away from fulfilling my New Year's resolution."

"Bully for you."

"Maybe there's something in this New Year's resolution business, Ted. Resolving to do something may be half the battle if you really mean it. You ought to try it sometime—maybe on that by-line you always wanted."

At that moment the only resolution Ted could think of was to get as far away as he could from Forestdale, from the newspaper office, and from Mr. Halliday. The miles quickly mounting on the speedometer were rapidly fulfilling this resolution.

"Thanks. I'll try to remember next year."

* * * *

Back at the *Town Crier* office, Mr. Dobson had read Ted's story several times. He placed it back on the desk, and removed his glasses.

"How is it?" asked Miss Monroe.

"Hm?" Mr. Dobson mused, recollecting his thoughts. "Oh, the story. Fine, fine. It's odd, though—in a big city readers would think it sort of corny, but in a small town like this I think it's just about right. Ted not only tells what Mr. Halliday did, but why, in such a way that you can't help feeling sorry for the man. I'm going to print the story just the way Ted wrote it. By rights, I ought to rewrite it and make it a little more impersonal, but I don't want to tamper with the feeling Ted put into it."

"The strike?" his secretary questioned.

"Oh, this story will settle the strike, all right—at least until next contract time. It wasn't really a dispute over issues as much as it was a clash of personalities—Mr. Abbott's and Mr. Prentice's. Now that they know where the friction was coming from, they'll settle quickly."

"But if Ted's story settles the strike," his secretary pointed out, "then it really was a big story—the biggest story Ted's ever handled."

"Oh, yes, it's a big story, all right, even though I know Ted isn't very proud of it." He hesitated. "Ted was hurt about all of this, but he'll get over this knock more or less. Still it remains in the back of your mind. After you get enough of them, you eventually turn into a hard-bitten old editor like me."

He smiled a little, not quite meaning what he said, but not exactly *not* meaning it, either. He sighed, readjusted his glasses, and picked up a pencil. At the top of Ted's story he printed neatly: "By Ted Wilford." Then he tossed the paper into the wire basket, where it would later be picked up by the printer.

www.ingramcontent.com/pod-product-compliance
Lightning Source LLC
Chambersburg PA
CBHW020657180626
46816CB00003B/1331